Historical Novels FOR
ENGAGING THINKERS

THIS BOOK BELONGS TO:

_____

_____

TO COLLIN

The Jeweled Astrolabe

Published by

BRIMWOOD PRESS

1941 Larsen Drive
Camino, California 95709
www.brimwoodpress.com

Text copyright © 2008 Jennifer Johnson Garrity
Cover illustrations by Kelsey Garrity copyright © 2008 by BrimWood Press
Book illustrations copyright © 2008 Lee Fitzgerrell Smith
Book design by Carmen Pereira Pucilowski

Printed in the United States of America
First Edition

Library of Congress Control Number: 2008923076
ISBN: 978-0-9770704-6-6

THE JEWELED ASTROLABE

An Historical Novel for Engaging Thinkers

JENNIFER JOHNSON GARRITY
Cover illustration by KELSEY GARRITY
Text illustrations by LEE FITZGERRELL SMITH

Other
HISTORICAL NOVELS FOR ENGAGING THINKERS
by the same author:

The Secret Scribe, *Ancient*

Beneath the Cat's Claw, *Early Modern*

Rebel on the Path, *Modern*

Medieval Europe

12TH CENTURY

Paris

Ottmarsheim

Cluny

Charnay

Lyon

Marseilles

Toledo

al-Andalus (Sefard)

Cordoba

Cadiz

Fez

al-Maghrib

Marrakesh

Rhine River

Saône River

Rhône River

Guadalquivir River

Black Forest

Bohemia

Ellwangen
Ulm
• Augsburg
Mengen

Constantinople

Silk Road

Levant

Cordoba, Spain - 1142

Gavriel ben Solomon Zafrani slackened his pace as he left the broad street and entered a narrow alley. Why should I hurry toward the worst part of the day? he thought. He would rather reverse his steps and dawdle at home, watching his mother and Mira do Sabbath cleaning. He would even rather return to school – if only he could! It was funny, how the boys there envied him. For the past year and a half, since he turned thirteen, only five hours of study per day had been required of him. While those boys who were destined to become teachers or rabbis remained bent over *Torah* and *Talmud* until the time of evening prayer, Gavriel was set free. But for what?

Blood and vomitus. The putrid stench of urine and festering wounds and sores. The stringent odor of sour wine and medicinal powders.

Gavriel understood that there was great honor in becoming a physician. It was an illustrious career, one that would one day take him into princely courts and pay him well. His father, Solomon ben Judah

Zafrani, had definitely earned the Arabic title of Hakim. Wise One. Learned One. A physician to be sought after by the most powerful people in _al-Andalus_. But where was it written that a son must follow in his father's footsteps? Whenever he asked that question he received the same short reply:

"Because in our family, it has always been so."

This was true not only of the Zafrani family, but other families as well. Akiva the _shohet's_ son would certainly become a _kosher_ butcher like his father, slaughtering animals in accordance with Jewish law. Like Gavriel, Akiva was now released early from school in order to become better acquainted with his future profession. And little Moses Maimon, only six years old, was already slated to become a rabbi like his father. The elder Maimon bragged long and often about all the clever things the boy said, predicting a glorious future for him.

But Gavriel's own father had stopped bragging some time ago.

Perhaps he'd stopped the first time Gavriel turned greenish-white during a simple boil lancing procedure, and had to sit down, gasping for air to keep from fainting. Or maybe he'd stopped five months ago, when a gardener had entered the dispensary with a half-severed toe, on which he'd dropped a sharp axe. Told to remove the patient's filthy, blood-soaked sandal, Gavriel had failed miserably. At the feel of the warm, sticky fluid on his fingers he had backed abruptly away, upsetting a small table, sending clean surgical knives onto the floor and shattering a _cupping glass_.

Solomon had not become angry over the incident. But around that time he began to wear a perpetual disappointed expression, which he tried to hide behind a patient smile.

Gavriel inhaled one last, deep breath of cool February air before entering the dispensary. Inside, offensive odors assaulted his nostrils. The stone walls and ancient mosaic floor of the building seemed to have absorbed the stench of urine over the centuries, only to sweat it out in the heat of each new day. As always, the waiting room was crammed with patients. They squatted against the walls or sprawled on *esparto* mats. It was not his father, but Solomon's fellow hakim, Zahid al-Jady, who met Gavriel, the loose folds of his *khamisa* billowing with the speed of his stride.

"Salaam, Gavriel. You are late; go quickly to your father. There is an especially bad bone break."

If al-Jady saw the look of dread creep across the boy's face, he ignored it. The tall, graceful hakim turned abruptly toward the medicinals table, pulling at his pointed black beard like he always did when puzzling over something. Near Gavriel's feet, a woman moaned in pain and thrashed wildly on a scrap of worn, woolen carpet. Though her face was veiled, by her blue eyes Gavriel could see she was a *Berber*. Her worried husband crouched beside her, murmuring prayers.

Solomon's examination room opened off the inner courtyard. Its whitewashed walls and smooth, stone floor remained cool, even in the most vicious heat. Hakim Zafrani glanced up with relief at his son's arrival. His black caftan was soaked with the sweat of the patient on the table, and he held a small vial of liquid. A smile glinted between his graying mustache and full beard.

He spoke Hebrew to his son, as always. "*Shalom*, Gavriel."

Quickly Gavriel assessed the scene before him. A youth with tear-stained face, not much younger than Gavriel, lay on the table, one knee swollen into a bluish-red lump. "Shall I hold him for you, Father?"

Solomon, propping up the boy's head and pouring a mouthful of *hemp* and barley water between his lips, replied, "No. This is as good an opportunity as any for you to learn to set bone fragments. The kneecap is shattered."

A sickening lump rose in Gavriel's throat.

"Come along; let me guide your hand." Solomon laid the youth's head gently down and took his son's reluctant hand. "Now feel carefully for the loose fragments beneath the skin. Count them."

The patient groaned miserably as Gavriel's clumsy fingers probed the injury.

"It's swollen. I can't tell where one bone fragment begins and another ends."

Solomon lifted his son's hand from the knee. "Gavriel, these fingers are capable of seeing beneath the skin. You must be patient. It will not happen instantly; take your time and concentrate."

Drawing a deep breath of resolve, Gavriel started again. He could feel a large fragment – the lower half of the kneecap. Above it, a smaller piece of bone had twisted sideways and now jutted sharply against the skin. He was afraid to touch that one. Another piece moved beneath his fingers, but he couldn't tell if it was out of place or in its proper spot. Trying to determine this, he pressed hard, his hand slipped, and his wristbone jabbed into the knee.

"_Allah_, have mercy!" screamed the patient, writhing in pain.

Solomon poured another gulp of barley-hemp water into his grimacing mouth.

"Try again in a minute," he urged. "Gavriel, you _must_ learn this procedure."

"_I'll_ do it."

Father and son both looked up, startled. It was Nizar, Hakim al-Jady's sixteen- year-old son. Tall and slender like his father, he was dressed in a spotless white khamisa and had damp hair, as if he had just come from a refreshing dip at a bathhouse. "What is it? A broken femur?"

"A kneecap," said Solomon, switching effortlessly into Arabic.

"Splendid! I can do it."

With supreme confidence, Nizar examined the shattered kneecap, his eyes closed, his lips pursed in concentration. Gavriel watched his face intently. The Arab's smooth forehead wrinkled thoughtfully above eyebrows far thicker than his newly sprouting mustache.

"Only the lower half is intact. I feel at least five fragments above, though not all are clean breaks. No, wait ... a sixth fragment!"

"Well done, Nizar," Solomon said. "Gavriel, you may hold the patient steady."

Gavriel slipped behind the young man's head and looped his arms around his armpits.

"That's it ... you've got it, Nizar," Solomon coached. "Turn it, turn it ... yes!"

Through a blur of tears, Gavriel watched Nizar's agile fingers coax the wayward bone pieces into their

proper positions. The patient, in whom the hemp
water had begun to take effect, still moaned but no
longer struggled.

"And now, what kind of splint is needed?"
Solomon asked Nizar.

"A double splint," the youth replied, "rigid and
tightly fastened. It should be made of hardwood
– oak or olive."

"Correct!"

When the splint was applied and Nizar had
breezed off to his next patient, Solomon said to
Gavriel, "Remember, he is two years older than you.
There is no reason why you might not, one day, do all
that he does – and with equal skill."

Gavriel nodded, noticing as he did so that the
patient had at last slipped into an exhausted slumber.
For a moment Gavriel considered the possibility of
drinking barley-hemp water and telling his father he
was feeling ill and needed to go home. But looking up
and seeing Solomon's dark eyes reading his face, he
asked merely, "What do you want me to do next?"

The dispensary was full to bursting. Whole
families lingered, anxious over a child's fever or ache.
Solitary men of every kind – Jew, Arab, Christian
– waited, some finely dressed, most ragged and
crawling with lice, each with a complaint. Here was
a sharp pain in the side, there a racking cough, or a
swollen, stiff joint. Gavriel shadowed first his father,
then al-Jady, watching them cleanse deep cuts with
wine and sew them up with human hair, listening to
them thoroughly quiz each patient about his symptoms. He helped al-Jady place a tourniquet around

the arm of an elderly man, but when the hakim opened a vein and began to draw blood, Gavriel's legs went wobbly at the knees and he had to leave the room.

It wasn't that he didn't want to heal people, he reflected as he sat watching the water bubbling in the courtyard fountain. His grandfather, great-grandfather and countless ancestors before them had practiced medicine here in Cordoba. When, back in the time of the Romans, the first Zafranis had left the _Levant_ and traveled westward to Spain – this lush and lovely land the Arabs called al-Andalus and the Jews called _Sefarad_ - they had no doubt disembarked from a Roman _galley_ carrying medicinal powders and surgical instruments. Gavriel had been born to carry on the Zafrani family tradition; he was the only son among four sisters. The importance of this he well understood. Why, then, had he also been born with such a weak stomach?

He felt a hand on his shoulder and glanced up into Solomon's face. The physician's black caftan reeked of spilled wine and sweat, with a faint hint of the mutton fat soap with which he scrubbed his hands between patients.

"When the Almighty formed me inside my mother," Gavriel grumbled miserably, "couldn't he have made my stomach strong and my nose not quite so sensitive?"

With a weary sigh, Solomon sat down beside his son, allowing himself a rare few moments' rest. He massaged tired eyes with one hand. "Gavriel, I do not understand your difficulties, because they have never been mine. I was raised in this dispensary and loved it from my earliest days. I only know that there is no higher calling for a man than to heal the sick, unless it is to be a rabbi. Do you want to become a rabbi, my son?"

Gavriel stared into the water, shaking his head. Five hours daily of Torah and Talmud study was more than enough for him. If he had to pore over the holy books from morning 'til night he would go crazy. He wanted to move, not sit.

"If you were a fourth, third, or even a second son, I would send you to Seville and apprentice you to a mapmaker, or a gold- or silversmith here in Cordoba. I might even say, 'Come, then; learn to be a shoemaker or a tailor,' though such professions are beneath the dignity of our family. But you are a first son ... an *only* son. Though it is difficult for you, I cannot bring myself to allow you to abandon our family profession."

"And your own brothers?" Gavriel said. "They are not all physicians."

"True," conceded Solomon. The hakim came from a large family of boys, which Gavriel suspected made it especially disappointing for him to have fathered only one male child. "But two of my brothers *are* physicians, along with me. Because of that, the younger ones were allowed to follow other paths."

Behind them, al-Jady's voice floated out of an examination room as he discussed a patient's symptoms with his son. Nizar was listening attentively, cutting in now and then with an "I see," and an astute observation of his own.

"Nizar was created to be a physician," said Gavriel with no jealousy or resentment in his voice. He admired Nizar, *liked* him even. The Arab hakim and his son were both friendly and warm, if a bit arrogant. Zahid al-Jady, a descendent of some of the first Arabians to arrive in al-Andalus, had worked alongside Solomon for years. They understood each other completely. The two families exchanged gifts on both Jewish and Muslim holidays and often dined together.

"And believe it or not, so were you," Solomon insisted stubbornly. "It just so happens that your road to becoming a hakim is more treacherous than Nizar's. That means when you arrive, we will have all the more reason to celebrate, and you will bring something extra with you into the world of medicine – determination."

He left Gavriel alone by the fountain.

Why won't he give up on me? thought the boy. A child's harsh, hacking cough reminded him that there was work to be done. Rousing himself, he returned to the bustle of the dispensary.

Late that afternoon, Solomon and Gavriel changed out of their work caftans and put on clean ones. It was summer; sundown and the beginning of Sabbath were still hours away, but there were errands to run as well as the required visit to the bathhouse.

Al-Jady and his own son were leaving also, bound for Friday evening prayers at the mosque.

"That's all for today!" announced Solomon to the waiting crowd. "Hakim al-Jady will return tomorrow morning, and I will return on Sunday."

Sighs of disappointment echoed around the room. The remaining patients were mostly *Mozarab* Christians who felt no compulsion to leave early on a Friday afternoon.

"We've waited since noon!" shouted an elderly man with a scaly face rash. "Can't you stay?"

"My religion forbids it." Solomon spoke with the patience of a man who has grown used to explaining such things.

"What about the Muslim doctor?" asked a teenage boy with a swollen foot.

Al-Jady glanced backward from the medicine table, where he and Nizar were giving their hands a final scrubbing.

"Please examine my daughter!" pleaded a Christian Mozarab woman on the verge of tears. Dressed in the rough clothing of farmers, she and her husband looked weary and bedraggled, as if they had made an arduous journey from the far countryside into Cordoba. "One of her eyes is swollen shut!"

Solomon and al-Jady exchanged glances. Nizar caught Gavriel's eye and rolled his toward the ceiling to show his irritation. The two fathers and their sons drew together to confer. With a deep sigh, Solomon said, "For some reason, there always seems to be more illness on Friday than on other days."

Zahid al-Jady put a hand on Solomon's shoulder. "Take your son and go. Nizar and I have already been to the mosque today for noon prayer. We will say our evening prayers here in the courtyard and attend to the patients."

"My friend, you are a good soul. And I will do the same for you on any day of your choice next week – except the Sabbath!"

Gavriel accompanied Nizar to the corner where two prayer rugs were kept rolled up. He helped Nizar spread them on the courtyard ground.

"I'm sorry you have to stay, Nizar."

The Arab youth dragged tired fingers through his black hair. "It isn't your fault. If these Christians had their own physicians ... "

"Does such a thing even exist? A Christian physician?"

Nizar laughed, "I'll give you one silver _dirham_ for every Christian doctor you find me in all of al-Andalus!"

Gavriel laughed along with him, but as he and his father left the dispensary, closing the heavy wooden door and turning away those patients lined up in the alley, he couldn't help feeling that if he had pulled his weight here today, more people would have been treated and the al-Jadys would not be working late.

CHAPTER TWO

Solomon and Gavriel hurried through a maze of alleys toward the Jewish bath house. A blind and wizened doorman admitted them. At the sound of a few dirhams clinking in his open palm, he stepped aside, offering thanks in Hebrew. Hastily, father and son shed their clothes and entered a cloud of steam. Wood smoke flavored the air, from the roaring fires heating cauldrons of water. Through the thick, white atmosphere Gavriel listened to the familiar murmur of men and boys taking part in the ancient Hebrew cleansing ritual. Some of his friends were there, but it was a Sabbath eve, and there was no time to linger. Home must be reached before sunset.

They scrubbed themselves in the tepid water, dressed and made their way to the synagogue. The _hazzan_ had already begun to chant the Sabbath prayers, his melodious voice floating out to meet the new arrivals. At the entrance to the sacred building, they shed their shoes. The feel of the cool marble floor against the soles of his feet made Gavriel shiver.

Yet as he placed his feet neatly together, bowing his head and repeating after the hazzan, the voices of his fellow Jews and their familiar ritual wrapped him in a contented warmth. While praying, he peeked up at the stone lions flanking the steps that led to the ark. In his childhood they had frightened him. Now they were like old friends – constant, loyal, guarding the sacred scrolls that lay at the heart of a Jew's worship. Each time Gavriel went forward to kiss those scrolls, he delighted in those lions and the luminous glow of the gold-embroidered curtains as they reflected the flame of the lamp burning before the ark.

On their way home from synagogue they passed through the market place.

"Fresh shad sounds delicious," mused Solomon as he hungrily inspected a fisherman's stall. "It is a good price and Mira knows how to prepare it to perfection. Your mother will be pleased."

"And honey almond pastries?"

"Yes, let's not forget those."

They arrived home a mere quarter of an hour before sundown. As Solomon had predicted, his wife Rohel was delighted with his Sabbath purchases. She was scrubbed and scented, dressed in a blue silk gown with green girdle tied around her hips. Her black hair was properly hidden beneath a silk scarf and her wrists jangled with the heavy gold jewelry she always wore on Sabbath eve.

"Now hurry, Solomon! Change into your slippers and put your medicine bag away before Sabbath arrives."

"Yes, Rohel," replied Solomon, as his wife

snatched the food and bustled toward the kitchen to give it to Mira.

Gavriel watched her disappear into the large, well-equipped kitchen. She was always rushing about during the final minutes before Sabbath arrived. He had very few memories of seeing her outside the stone walls of this house. The stately dwelling had belonged in her family for generations. It was her fortress. Rohel Santob Zafrani ruled over her home like a queen over an empire, and she seldom left its elegant rooms and shady courtyard except to go to synagogue and pray with other women behind the lace curtain.

Cordoba had once been the jewel of al-Andalus, the sparkling metropolis from which the _Caliphs_ ruled. But the grand, old city had seen one disaster after another during the last few centuries. One war after another had chipped away at its splendor. Then rough, uncouth Berber tribesmen from _al-Maghrib_ had sacked it, leaving much of it in ruins. Merino sheep now grazed on the grassy rubble where fine buildings formerly stood.

For the past sixty years, al-Andalus had been governed by the Veiled Ones. Their _Emir_ governed from distant Marrakesh in al-Maghrib, entrusting the day-to-day running of Cordoba and other Andalusian cities to his faithful Muslim followers. They were blue-eyed, fair-skinned Berbers, who called themselves _Almoravids_ and went about with a thick cloth covering their noses and mouths. Islamic law meant everything to them, and they strictly enforced it. This terrified those who were not Muslims.

Whole neighborhoods of Jews and Mozarabs had
fled the beloved city and resettled in the north,
where Christians ruled. But Rohel's family, the proud
Santobs, who owned mills and vineyards in the countryside surrounding Cordoba, had never considered
leaving. The Zafranis had also refused to flee, along
with a handful of other families. Now they formed
the backbone of a small but strong Jewish community, utterly devoted to Cordoba, their ancient home.

Rohel was as much a part of this house as
Solomon was a part of the dispensary. If Gavriel's
mother ever tired of staying shut up indoors, she
never complained. He knew she was safest inside,
away from the Almoravid soldiers who patrolled the
streets on horseback. Not only Jewish women, but
Jewish men, along with Christian men and women
in Cordoba did well these days to hurry about
their business and get off the streets as quickly as
possible.

Refreshed from his bath but still feeling miserable from his failure, Gavriel made straight for the
spacious inner room. Sixteen-year-old Nahum was
there with Ashira, Gavriel's fifteen-year-old sister.
The two were married, but they sat on silk cushions, across from one another like brother and sister,
contemplating a game of chess. The gold bracelets he
had given her at their wedding jangled as she moved
a silver rook across the wooden board. Gavriel's
younger sisters, Hinda, Yona and Nava, all freshly
scrubbed and dressed in their finest silks, hovered
nearby, watching the game.

"Shalom, Gavriel," said Nahum, never taking his

eyes off the board.

"Shalom."

Gavriel left them to their amusement and seated himself with a weary sigh in a far corner of the room.

"What happened?" asked Ashira over her shoulder. "Another bad day?"

"I don't want to talk about it."

"Isn't it happening a bit frequently," asked Nahum as he captured one of Ashira's pawns, "this moping about and looking miserable after you get home from the dispensary?"

Gavriel felt like hitting his brother-in-law. Nahum was the youngest son of a cloth merchant, a natural scholar who upon his marriage had left his own family's home to live with the Zafranis. Solomon and Rohel proudly supported him as he studied, knowing he would one day be a rabbi and Ashira a rabbi's wife. He was a theological nitpicker. Suited for long hours of study as a thoroughbred horse is suited to gallop across a grassy plain, Nahum had never shown any sympathy for Gavriel's plight.

"Gavriel," cooed tiny Nava, barely three. She toddled over and climbed on his lap. "Mira is cooking *pilah* for us!"

Gavriel shut Nahum out of his mind and turned his full attention to Nava's prattle.

Soon Mira entered with a tureen of fish stew. Mother followed with a tray of olives and pilah. Hastily she lit the oil lamps, then sat down beside her husband. "Gather round, everyone," she said. "The sun is setting."

Solomon placed his hands on each family

member's head and blessed them. Even the household slave, Mira, who had never given up wearing a carved wooden cross suspended from a leather cord around her neck, bowed her head and received the Sabbath blessing. When he had finished, she began ladling out the stew. Its spicy smell coaxed back the appetite Gavriel had lost earlier at the dispensary.

As bowls of rosewater were passed around and fingers dipped before eating, Solomon sang,

"This is the sanctified rest day
Happy the man who observes it
Thinks of it over his wine cup
Feeling no pang at his heartstrings...
Comes the sweet, restful Sabbath
Singing and joy in its footsteps
Light and rejoicing to Israel
Sabbath, the soother of sorrows,
Comfort of downtrodden Israel
Healing the hearts that were broken ...."

Mira, a *Slav* from Bohemia, hummed along. She had been part of the Zafrani household since before Gavriel's birth, when Solomon purchased her at a local slave market. The Jewish rituals were now as familiar to her as her own strange language, and she performed all the Sabbath chores as well as her regular weekly ones. She had an ear for foreign tongues, and spoke both Arabic and Hebrew admirably. Her mysterious Slavic tongue was used only to sing and mutter to herself while working, or to pray to Christ and various saints. Stout and with a ruddy complexion, she looked out of place in sunny al-Andalus, where most of the women were dark and slight of build. Even the Berber women's skin was deeply tanned, but Mira's remained white. If the hapless slave was ever unlucky enough to spend hours in the sun, it reddened and peeled like the crisp skin of a new potato.

Gavriel wondered if she ever dreamed of the distant Slav country on those rare moments when her work was done and she rested, alone in the courtyard beneath the shade of a palm tree. Or perhaps she remembered shivering on winter nights in an earthen-floored hut in a dark forest. Uncle Baruch, who dealt in slaves, had assured Solomon that the Slavonic people lived a squalid life in their cold, windswept country. He knew for a fact, he said, that they were happy to exchange Bohemia's muddy fields and snowy forests for the brilliant skies and paved streets of al-Andalus. Whether Mira felt so or not the Zafrani family could only guess, for she never spoke to them of anything beyond her household duties. Neither did they ask her her thoughts on such things.

After dinner, Gavriel laid aside his resentment and challenged Nahum to a game of chess. As Mira cleared away the clutter of the feast, the Zafrani family settled down on cushions and plush carpets to read, talk and enjoy goblets of spiced, fruity wine. Solomon selected a newly purchased paper volume of Arabic poems and took the younger girls on his lap to read to them in a low, sing-song voice. The Zafrani book cupboard boasted leather-bound medical journals as well as poetry, some ancient and made of vellum, containing the works of ancient Greek scholars such as Galen and Hippocrates. Like Ashira and Gavriel before them, the younger Zafrani children were daily taught to revere books and treat them with utmost care and respect.

Nahum, the only family member who could beat Gavriel at chess, quickly backed his opponent's king into a corner. Before Gavriel could capitulate and call for another round, a clatter in the street disrupted the game. Footsteps, voices and the loud clang of an iron doorknocker brought the whole family to the front of the house. Mira opened the door.

There, in the lamplit alley, stood an elegantly dressed man, freshly alighted from a sedan chair.

"Reuven!" Solomon leapt forward and caught his younger brother in a crushing embrace.

"The cloak, the cloak," squeaked Reuven, gasping for breath. "You'll crush the fur!"

Solomon backed away as Reuven brushed fussy hands over the black fox collar. "Please, show a little respect for the clothing. I paid a purse full of silver for this in Damascus."

After dropping coins into the porters' hands, Reuven turned to his servant, a lanky Arab in a dull brown tunic. "Aziz," he said with a nod toward the door, and the man immediately carried two bulging leather satchels inside the house.

Rohel clasped her brother-in-law's arm. "Welcome, Reuven! How glad we are to see you again. Come, drink some Sabbath wine with us."

The whole Zafrani family crowded around as Aziz lifted the fur-trimmed cloak from his master's shoulders. Beneath it Reuven sported a sleek black caftan embroidered with gold. Small Nava, mesmerized by the sparkling threads in his sleeve, took her uncle by the hand and led him into the sitting room. He made the rounds and kissed everyone's hand in greeting, leaving behind him a whisper of perfume. Finally, he settled himself on a cushion. Aziz removed Reuven's leather boots and retired to a corner to wait for whatever food or drink Mira might bring him. But before Mira could think of her fellow slave's needs, she scurried to bring a goblet of wine and a bowl of rosewater so that Solomon's brother could wash his hands.

"Ahh," Reuven sighed. He dipped his fingers in the refreshing liquid and brought them to his nose for an appreciative sniff. "It's good to be back in Sefarad!"

"But when...how...?" Solomon's brow wrinkled with too many questions at once.

"My ship docked on Monday in Cadiz. It took two days to find respectable Jews with which to leave my trade goods, and another two days to sail up the Guadalquivir River, thanks to a serious lack of breeze."

"And what brings you *here*, Uncle," Gavriel asked. "You never come to Cordoba just to see us. You must have a little business on the side."

"Clever boy," laughed Reuven, catching Gavriel's chin in one hand. "Is your father still determined to make a physician out of you?"

"I am indeed," replied Solomon before Gavriel could speak. "But enough of that. Tell us about your family."

"Devorah and the children are well," Reuven said. "But life in Fez..." he shrugged and moved his hands like two scales in the act of balancing. " A little joy, a little sorrow. Oh, whom am I trying to kid? Life is horrible in al-Maghrib. The Almoravids are putting more and more pressure on us Jews. Devorah stays mostly in the house because she's afraid to go outside. We try not to call attention to ourselves."

"Yes, I can see that," said Solomon, smiling ironically at the gigantic ruby ring on his brother's finger and the gold chain around his neck. "It's not easy here either, Reuven. The Almoravids have become increasingly self-righteous and brutal. They look with disgust on our Andalusian ways; they detest the way Jews, Arabs and Christians live side-by-side and work together here. You can imagine what that might one day mean for us at the dispensary."

Reuven nodded impatiently. "Yes, Solomon, I grew up here, remember? I know Andalusian life under the Almoravids, but I'm telling you, it's ten times worse down there in al-Maghrib." With a furtive glance at Aziz, he lowered his voice, although the Arabic slave surely had no understanding of Hebrew. "And if you think the Almoravids are bad, you should see the _Almohads_. They are gaining power in North Africa – a ruthless, intolerant lot. The Almohads believe in killing anyone who refuses to convert to Islam. Word has it they will overrun Marrakesh and invade al-Andalus sometime in the next decade. And when that happens ... brother, you don't want to be here in Cordoba."

"Is that why you came?" asked Gavriel. "To warn us?"

Reuven took a long sip of wine. "Partly. There are other reasons, all of which I'm not yet ready to divulge. But here is one of them: I plan to move my family out of Fez, and I have my sights set on Toledo."

Solomon and Rohel nodded in understanding. Many of the Jewish families that had abandoned Muslim-ruled Cordoba had fled north to Toledo.

"Live under Christian rule?" Nahum's upper lip curled in an incredulous sneer. "That would be like setting the clock back five hundred years!"

"True, my young nephew-in-law. Nevertheless, Jews have managed to make a good life for themselves up there, among those backward Christians. I don't care if I live among wolves and bears as long as they are willing to live peaceably with me, and apparently the Christians and Muslims in Toledo are willing to do just that. We Jews can't ask for more."

Solomon regarded his brother skeptically. "What are some of your other reasons for making this journey? Buying or selling something, perhaps?"

Throwing up both hands, Reuven sighed, "You know me only too well, brother. Spring is nearly here and yes, I'm once again setting off on a business trip. In fact, I'm on the way to the most spectacular sale of my career! And when I've completed that sale, I plan to stop in Toledo on the way home to buy a house for my family. Not just any house, mind you. When I sell what I have to sell, there will be enough gold in my purse to buy the grandest, most finely-crafted home in all of Spain!"

"What is it, Uncle Reuven? What are you selling?" Gavriel scooted closer, fastening his eyes on

Reuven's tanned, beardless face. A delicate scar ran alongside his finely shaped, pointed nose – a permanent reminder of an encounter with bandits on the _Silk Road_ five years earlier. Reuven ben Judah Zafrani, the youngest in a large family of brothers, had never been required to study medicine. Instead, possessing supreme self-confidence and a strong sense of adventure, he'd been crossing seas and deserts since his eighteenth year. He knew the streets and alleys of Jerusalem, Damascus and Constantinople as intimately as those of Cordoba and Fez. Twice he had even journeyed as far as Kai Feng Foo, where a colony of Jews had settled among the Mandarins and learned to breed silkworms.

Reuven spoke Hebrew and Arabic flawlessly. He also spoke enough Frankish, Andalusi and Latin to converse, and had even learned to bargain in the Mandarin tongue. He had traveled by camel caravan through places with magical names like Samarkhand and Tashkent. There was no desirable object that Uncle Reuven had not at one time bought, sold, or transported from east to west, north to south and back again. He had even been as far north as the Baltic Sea, where trading posts had emerged along the misty water's edge. There the Danes and Swedes plied the icy waters with their long boats, eager to trade their _amber_ and fur pelts for silks and spices. What more could Reuven possibly wish to see in this world? He had already covered it from end to end.

"I have my usual ells of silk. I have nutmeg and cinnamon, medicinal powders and perfumes," disclosed Reuven. "But this time I also have something to sell, the likes of which no one in this room has ever seen."

"Try us," said Nahum skeptically.

Reuven gave the boy a haughty glance. "It's an _astrolabe_."

"An astrolabe?" snorted Nahum. "Who in al-Andalus hasn't seen an astrolabe?" Ashira looked at her husband and rolled her eyes. The instrument for charting stars and planets was certainly nothing new in the Arab and Jewish world.

"You've never seen one like _this_," said Reuven. He reached beneath his caftan and opened a linen sack he kept strapped to his belly.

CHAPTER THREE

CHAPTER III

Reuven was right. No one in the room had ever seen an astrolabe like it. Its sturdy brass disc had been overlaid with silver; its engraved, circular lines were inlaid with gold. The pointers were carved of ivory and encrusted with rubies and sapphires.

"Magnificent!" gasped Ashira, her brown eyes gleaming. She reached out to touch it.

Reuven snatched it away protectively. "Yes, isn't it? It was made in Fez. And though you smart-alecks have seen an astrolabe or two in your day, even the simplest of astrolabes is still a rarity in the Christian north."

"But surely in Toledo ... "

"I'm not talking about Toledo, Solomon. I'm talking about the Rhinelands. On my last trip to the Levant, I met a German _bishop_ on pilgrimage to Jerusalem. Oh, he traveled in style, that one, flanked by mounted soldiers and an endless train of servants! We got to talking. The talk turned to astrolabes, and he mentioned he wanted to purchase one as a gift for the Benedictine abbey at Ellwangen. Since I had already seen this one in the making, I described it to him. His eyes glittered. 'I will spare no expense,' he said, and so I promised to deliver it this summer. He, in turn, promised to send funds to the _abbot_ at Ellwangen so that he can pay me on my arrival."

Ever cautious, Solomon asked, "And if the abbot doesn't receive the funds? If the bishop forgets or changes his mind?"

"No worries. There are plenty of other abbots and bishops in the Rhinelands whose eyes would pop at the sight of this fabulous instrument. The Christian world is just beginning to wake up to the fact that there is such a thing as scientific study. Those few inquisitive ones among them are hungry for our Andalusian knowledge." Reuven slapped his forehead in dramatic disgust and leaned toward his elder brother. "Solomon, they don't even practice decent medicine up there!"

"What do you expect?" said Nahum acidly. "They're _Christians_."

Solomon gave his young son-in-law a reproving look. "That isn't the reason they're ignorant, Nahum. We would live in ignorance, too, if we labored under the same brutal system that traps them."

"My brother always did have a heart for the downtrodden," muttered Reuven.

Solomon ignored the comment and seized the opportunity to instruct Gavriel. "Son, remember this each time a Christian walks into our dispensary – there would be more Christian physicians if Christians had such things as schools for higher learning."

"That's exactly what I've been saying!" protested Reuven.

Solomon held his eyes on Gavriel's face. "My brother spoke of the Rhinelands. The Rhinelanders and the Franks had a powerful king once. King Charles united a vast kingdom and dreamed of educating his people – even the peasants! He went so far as to set up free schools in monasteries across his empire. Unfortunately, the kings who followed him lacked his strength and vision, and before long his empire was carved into pieces. Monasteries are still storehouses of knowledge, but children no longer come to learn."

"Ignorance breeds ignorance," muttered Nahum.

Solomon fixed the arrogant scholar with a reproachful gaze. "You would be ignorant too, Nahum, if you were forced to labor all day in the fields of some lord's manor."

Duly chastened, Nahum lowered his head and retreated to sit beside Ashira.

Solomon turned back to Gavriel. "And as for *medicine*, Christian monks grow herbs and try their best to treat illness with them, but they simply do not have the resources that we Jews and Arabs take for granted."

Reuven, growing impatient with his brother's instructive speech, cut in. "I tell you, brother, you could make a fortune treating kings and high Churchmen up there...."

Solomon laughed and shook his head. He waved a hand as if shooing away the temptation to turn every conversation into a lesson. "I'll stay here in

31

Sefarad, thank-you."

Reuven regarded him with affectionate disdain.
"Well, that doesn't surprise me. Probably you'd stay
in Cordoba if it fell down around you and you were
the only thing left standing."

Gently, Gavriel coaxed the jeweled astrolabe

out of Reuven's hands and held it on his lap. Ashira scooted close and stared at it over his shoulder. He ran his fingers over the framework and gazed at the largest ruby until his eyes blurred. The luminous pink stone split into fragments that criss-crossed in his vision. Sinking deep into another world, he tried to envision life on the road, on the sea, on horseback. Uncle Reuven's hands touched finely spun silk, gold and jewels, amber, smooth glass vials of perfume. They sifted through exotic red-gold spices, while Solomon handled scabied skin, gaping, pus-filled wounds, stinking urine and blood. The life of a fifth son seemed far more enjoyable than that of a first.

Because a fifth son, decided Gavriel, *has much more freedom in life than a first son – or an only son.*

Another commotion in the street turned heads toward the front door. Reuven instinctively snatched the astrolabe and secured it in the pouch beneath his caftan. Before Solomon could rise from his cushion, Mira opened the door and two soldiers from the governor's palace strode into the room. They carried long, curved swords. Silver-handled daggers glinted in the sashes of their tunics. Their helmets were wrapped with dark red turbans, from which hung veils that obscured nose and mouth.

Reuven leaned close to Gavriel. "These Berbers," he whispered, "think they are still in the deserts of al-Maghrib, where sand will blow in their nostrils."

"Hakim Solomon Zafrani?"

The physician rose awkwardly, heavy with feasting. "I am Solomon."

"Governor Tashfin has taken ill. He has sent for

you to attend to him."

Gavriel stiffened, waiting for his father's certain reply.

"My friends, I regret to say it is impossible for me to attend to the governor tonight, and even tomorrow."

The two soldiers darted incredulous looks at one another over their face veils. "You *refuse* to come with us?" asked the more muscular of the two.

Nahum scooted closer to Ashira. Rohel slipped a protective arm around Hinda and Nava.

Solomon explained, "As the governor must surely know, my religion forbids me to work on the Hebrew Sabbath. Our Sabbath lasts from sunset on Friday to sunset on Saturday. If you would send for me tomorrow evening, or even Sunday, I ... "

"I told you he wouldn't come," said the thinner soldier to his companion. "I told you we should fetch al-Jady or another Arab doctor."

"Governor Tashfin asked specifically for Zafrani the Jew doctor!" snapped the muscular one. "Are we to ignore his wishes and bring whomever we wish?"

Solomon took advantage of the squabble and approached the guards with a disarming smile. "Come come, fellows – describe for me the governor's symptoms."

They exchanged uncertain glances before the thin one divulged, "All we know is what we were told to tell you: that he's feverish, he coughs, and his head aches."

"Does the cough rattle in his chest, or is it dry, and hacking?" The seasoned physician guided the soldiers inside and offered them seats. Both men helped themselves to the sweet wafers sitting on a silver tray.

The Zafrani family sat in strained silence as Solomon put forth question after carefully phrased question. Gavriel studied the carved hilt of the thin soldier's sword until he became aware of the man's contemptuous gaze upon him. The little mound of dried blood in the middle of his forehead revealed this soldier's devotion to Islam; it was a sign that he prayed with his face to the ground five times a day. He wore the scab proudly.

"If his excellency Governor Tashfin will drink a mixture of castoreum and crushed celery seed," instructed Solomon, "and wrap himself warmly, though he be hot and sweating, I am certain the sickness will run its course. Within two or three days his fever will break. In any case, I will gladly come to him when the Sabbath has ended."

At a look from Solomon, Mira brought his satchel from another room. With steady hands she measured out portions as he instructed her, mixing powders in a glass vial and sealing it with a stopper of wax.

"His religion forbids him even to mix his own medicines!" scoffed the scabbed Berber.

The other one muttered, "You Jews think you can defy even the Almoravid governor! Let me remind you that Allah has placed you under the authority of the One True Religion. Sooner or later you will be forced to bow to Islam."

Solomon did not respond. His face stiff as a

mask, he held out the vial of medicine, obviously waiting for the soldiers to take it and leave. They did so grudgingly, looking disappointed that no one had challenged them and given them a reason to wield their swords. At last they spun on their sandals and strode out into the alley.

When the door closed and Solomon turned to face his family, he was pale and trembling. A shiver crept down the back of Gavriel's neck.

"You see? It's coming here too!" exclaimed Reuven. "Like a scorching wind across the water ... the fanatical Almohads are reaching their grasping fingers into al-Andalus."

"Be quiet Reuven!" snapped Solomon.

"Solomon, the Sabbath is no time for harsh words," chided Rohel.

Reuven ignored them both. He paced the room, extending pleading hands to anyone who dared look him in the eye. "I'm telling you, things will only get worse. It's already gotten much worse! When I disembarked here in Cordoba last evening I sensed so little of the friendly atmosphere I knew as a child. It's not anything like it was back in our grandfathers' day, when the Caliphs ruled. Now *those* were fair and merciful Muslims! The Almoravids have turned this place into a harsh wasteland, and if the Almohads come ... I don't even want to think about what that will mean for all of you!"

Solomon gave his brother a stern, unblinking stare. "Reuven, you are ruining our Sabbath."

The handsome young trader sighed and dropped his head. "All right, all right; I'll be quiet."

His ringed fingers smoothed the folds of his caftan. "Forget I ever said a word."

Everyone sat down again, each trying to appear relaxed. Nahum nudged Ashira and they began a game of chess. The talk gradually turned to more pleasant subjects, but Gavriel longed to be alone with his uncle and ply him with questions.

ༀ   ༀ   ༀ

When, on Sunday morning, a sedan chair arrived to carry Solomon to the governor's palace, Gavriel and Uncle Reuven followed on foot. Reuven glanced uneasily at the escort of four armed soldiers marching alongside. "Your father is obviously respected and sought out by the wealthy and powerful in Cordoba. Tell me, Gavriel, why doesn't he spend most of his time treating such people?"

Gavriel pondered this as he kept pace behind the perspiring sedan porters. "I suppose because of *mitzvah*. A holy Jewish life. Obedience to God's law, acts of kindness, caring for those in need, and all that."

"And why else?" Reuven slapped his forehead in mock surprise. "Money my brother has enough of, from both his own and your mother's inheritance. But I just can't understand anyone whose heart doesn't race at the thought of earning more." Reuven chuckled. "And for the sake of mitzvah, my brother would rather treat the poor."

"It's always been like that. We work at the dispensary on Sunday, Monday, Tuesday and Friday. We visit the Jewish Inn on Wednesday and the Muslim *maristan* on Thursday. When a government official or a wealthy patient need father, they send for him."

"Do you know," asked Reuven, "what a prince in the Frankish kingdom or the Rhinelands would pay to have a Jewish physician constantly standing by to treat him?"

"My father will never leave al-Andalus, if that's what you're getting at."

"I wish he would," said Reuven. "But will he listen to me? The Almohads will give him a choice between converting to Islam, or death – exile, if he's lucky. Which is why I plan to move my family to Toledo."

The two fell silent, their cork-soled sandals moving in perfect sync. After a while, Reuven asked, "And you, Gavriel? Do you feel called to a life of healing the sick for the sake of mitzvah rather than money?"

Gavriel heaved a sigh. "Money isn't my problem."

"Oh? Is there a problem?"

"Yes, a big one. I ... "

A woman's shriek cut him off. Ahead in the road a party of horsemen escorted a group of prisoners toward the broad plaza where public punishment was meted out. Roped to one another at the wrists and ankles, the men shuffled along, barefoot and filthy from long days and nights in the squalor of their prison cells. A woman, perhaps the wife or sister of the last prisoner in line, tried to clutch at his arm but was shoved roughly to the ground by a soldier.

"Don't take his hand off!" she cried.

"Almoravid justice," muttered Reuven under his breath. "Steal a little something, and get your hand sliced off."

Sickened, Gavriel kept his eyes on the ground. "We see them in the dispensary ... afterward, when they need treatment for the infections caused by such 'justice.'"

"I'll take my chances with the Christians," said Reuven.

⁊ᶜ ⁊ᶜ ⁊ᶜ

The governor of Cordoba lived in a splendid stone palace built during the time of the Caliphs. Six veiled and turbaned guards stepped aside to allow the medical party passage into the courtyard. Their eyes followed the Jews' every move.

Governor Tashfin lay wrapped in a woolen blanket on his bed, in full accordance with Solomon's instructions. Damp hair clung to his forehead and his blue eyes were bloodshot. Unwrapping him, Solomon found him bare-chested and wearing a sweat-soaked breechcloth. As he had predicted, the governor's fever had broken.

The physician tapped up and down the patient's chest with short, firm blows, listening for unusual sounds. He pulled open the man's eyelids, and peered into his ears and mouth. "Gavriel, I need your assistance," he called softly.

Reuven watched his nephew shuffle reluctantly to Solomon's side.

"Can you cough something up for us?" the doctor asked Tashfin.

Gavriel extracted a glazed pottery dish from Solomon's leather satchel, resigned to the unpleasant task ahead. Positioning it below the governor's mouth, he closed his eyes and waited. With a rumbling cough followed by a series of hacks, the governor deposited a wad of phlegm in the bowl.

"Very good!" said Solomon.

Tashfin looked pleased with himself.

"Gavriel, what of the color?"

The boy pried one eye open. "Greenish-yellow."

"More green than yellow?"

He pried open the other eye as a familiar nausea welled up inside him. "No. Just the opposite."

"What, then, do you recommend?"

Gavriel closed his eyes and thought hard. "Castoreum. A mixture of rue gum and ... and ... "

"Stinking asafetida."

"Yes." In truth, Gavriel had known what to say, but found speech difficult when his stomach was reeling.

He helped Solomon mix the powders and pound them into a gum with mortar and pestle. After the paste was dissolved in warm honey water, the governor gulped it down and settled wearily back on a mountain of pillows.

"Since you are here, Zafrani," Governor Tashfin rasped, "I must tell you that my chief steward, al-Biham, has not been feeling well. He has lost weight, and suffers from an excessive thirst. Lately he complains of blurred vision."

Solomon listened carefully, his fingers stroking his beard. "My first inclination, in such a case, would be to examine him thoroughly, and inspect his urine."

Governor Tashfin immediately dispatched a servant to fetch the chief steward. When the slight man with the well-trimmed beard arrived, Tashfin said, "Al-Biham, you are to be examined. Take off your clothes!"

The chief steward's eyes darted around the room in alarm. At least ten servants were gathered around, not to mention a handful of government officials and Uncle Reuven, who had no good reason to be there.

"Hurry up. Don't waste the Jew physician's time!" barked the governor before plunging into a coughing fit.

The poor steward took a deep breath and disrobed down to his breechcloth. To Gavriel, Solomon gave the task of running both hands down the man's arms, legs and torso, feeling for lumps and other abnormalities. As his son did this, Solomon plied the man with the usual questions about his eating, sleeping and exercise habits. He posed endless questions about the man's parents' and grandparents' health, while not only the governor, but everyone else in the room listened intently. Finally Solomon nudged Gavriel and glanced meaningfully at his satchel. Gavriel knew what he wanted. Taking another glazed cup from the bag, the boy handed it to the patient.

"A sample of urine, please."

The steward paled, then turned bright red. "Right now? Here?"

"Go on, Al-Biham," ordered the governor.

"There's nothing to be ashamed of. Solomon Zafrani is the finest Jew-doctor in Cordoba."

Resigned to the loss of what little dignity he had left, the steward shuffled off to one corner, turned his back to the assembled crowd, and obeyed.

Gavriel gazed pleadingly at his father. Solomon returned his look with sympathy, but stern determination. He directed the patient to hand the sample to Gavriel.

The boy shot an agonized look at his uncle, who dropped his eyes discreetly to the floor.

"What of the amount?" asked Solomon.

"There is much."

"And the color?"

Gavriel peered into the cup. "It is a medium yellow."

"No blood?"

"No trace of it, Father."

"What of the consistency?"

Gavriel shook the cup until its contents gently swirled. "Cloudy."

"The odor?

Slowly Gavriel lowered his nose to the bowl. *If I do this part well enough,* he thought, *I might escape what's coming.* He despised the smell of urine, yet the odious substance was one of the most valuable tools for a physician, for it came from inside the body, bringing forth secrets otherwise hidden. "It smells ... it smells ... sweet."

He hadn't wanted to say it, but it was true, and now he knew he could not avoid the thing he dreaded.

Chapter Four

Solomon nodded in approval. "And what of the taste?"

Reuven scowled in disgust, his eyes filling with pity for his young nephew. With trembling hands, Gavriel brought the bowl toward his face. Fighting down his heaving stomach, he poked a reluctant tongue out of tight-pressed lips. The acrid yet sugary odor of the liquid wafted up his nostrils and filled his brain. It seemed to permeate his skin. The bowl's rim reached his chin but he could not will his hands to bring it any farther.

"Gavriel!"

Gavriel jerked the bowl up hard. Its contents sloshed over the edge and spilled down the front of his tunic. He froze in horror. Through clenched teeth he moaned, "I'm sorry ... I'm so sorry...."

Swiftly, Solomon grabbed the bowl and sniffed what liquid remained. He touched a bit of the urine to his tongue and pronounced, "It is the disease of over-sweetness."

A collective gasp rose from the onlookers as

Gavriel crumpled to the floor and vomited onto the cool mosaic tile. Through throbbing ears he heard the governor order a servant to clean up the mess. Lying there, weak and humiliated, he longed to disappear.

He was carried home in the sedan chair while Reuven and Solomon followed on foot. Gavriel could hear snatches of their conversation above the clatter in the streets.

"It's obvious to me, Solomon, that your son has no love of the medical profession."

"Sometimes duty comes first, and love creeps in later."

Reuven snorted, "And if it never creeps in?"

"Then mitzvah will have to suffice," Solomon replied.

"Ah, mitzvah, mitzvah," Reuven sighed.

🙦 🙦 🙦

Reuven spent a few days buying provisions for his journey, such as _matzoh_, salted kosher beef, dried figs and nuts. Otherwise he stayed at home, packing and repacking his bags, fussing over every detail, taking his time. Dawdling, even. Each evening when Gavriel returned home from the dispensary he expected Reuven to have departed, so eager was his uncle to get to the Rhinelands and close the deal on the astrolabe. Yet Reuven remained, lounging on cushions with his customary cup of spiced wine, chewing on dates or olives, saying, "I'll leave one of these days, when I've managed to find all the provisions I need for the journey."

No one minded. He caused no extra work, for his servant Aziz attended to his every whim. Reuven's presence made every meal seem like a Purim feast; he loved to tell jokes, and laugh uproariously at them. He quoted Hebrew poetry and sang Arabic love songs while strumming a guitar. He challenged everyone in the household to games of chess, even tiny Nava, patiently teaching her how to play. Not least, he regaled the family with hair-raising tales of his exploits on the Silk Road or in the Levant.

"The Levant is no place for a Jew these days," he declared one night, in a despairing tone. "May the Christian knights be cursed! Our father, may he rest, longed to see Jerusalem, but I'm telling you Solomon, I'm glad he never actually tried to go there."

Solomon, his eyelids sagging with the late hour, murmured, "The Holy One will avenge."

"Well, I wish he'd hurry up," Reuven snapped. "It's getting harder and harder to do business down there." He turned to Gavriel. "You should see it, boy – the streets of the Holy City crawling with *Templars*. They go where they please – drunk, and insulting women. They run roughshod over Muslim and Jew alike. They've erected shrines and churches willy-nilly, turning Jerusalem into their own private chapel. They pick up stones and nails and bits of wood, calling them sacred and practically worshipping them, saying Christ touched them. They trample the ancient streets on their bulky war horses, speaking Frankish and Latin, bellowing out drunken war songs. Last summer I had to disguise myself as a priest in order to get out of there alive!"

"Did you lose your goods?" gasped Rohel, caught up in the drama of it all.

A sly smile crept across her brother-in-law's face. "No, and here's why. Those Frankish bullies are not beyond taking bribes. Some knights in need of a few _deniers_ were only too happy to lead my donkeys out of the city and meet me on a back road to Bethlehem."

"You dressed as a priest!" exclaimed Nahum, unable to move beyond that shocking revelation.

Reuven retorted, "With permission from my rabbi! It's a common enough practice among Jewish travelers who want to save their skins. But then," he continued bitingly, "you scholars wouldn't know much about the real world out there, would you?"

Solomon chuckled and said with thinly veiled sarcasm, "Apparently business dealings are of the highest priority to the Almighty, Nahum. Jewish traders have a special place in his plan."

Reuven held up his wineglass for Aziz to refill. "Go ahead and laugh, Solomon. But what would you do without us? You certainly wouldn't be sitting on that elegant silk cushion. You wouldn't even have _camphor_, or opium to dull the pain of your patients."

"Brother, you have caught me!" laughed Solomon, raising both hands in surrender. "You speak the truth."

Reuven winked at Gavriel. "You see, even a great healer of men walks humbly on the earth and wants a little comfort and luxury."

Gavriel grinned. He adored his uncle. If only

Reuven would settle his family in Cordoba instead of Toledo! "There are probably Crusaders in Toledo, Uncle," he said, hoping to plant the idea in Reuven's mind.

"Not very many. Probably not any at all," said Reuven. "Such beasts will never be welcome in Spain. They're an insult to our way of life."

Solomon sighed and rose from his cushion. "Crusaders may not be welcome here in al-Andalus, but their handiwork is. The Jews and Muslims they've chased out of the Levant keep washing ashore here. The poor souls are hungry and homeless and many are sick. Most of them have spent their last bit of money to get here by ship. The Jews' Inn and the Muslim maristan are overflowing with them just now. Al-Jady and I have our hands full with these wanderers. But now I must sleep, and Gavriel too. The sick need us tomorrow like any other day."

🙙 🙙 🙙

"You may accept fees from the rich, my boys," Solomon instructed as he led Gavriel and Nizar along a narrow street toward the Jews' Inn. "But the poor we do not charge for our services. The poor must never be charged. If they insist on paying, they pay only what they can afford. Nizar, your father and I are in absolute agreement about this."

"Yes sir," Nizar replied, though these were things he had long ago learned at his own father's knee. Zafrani and al-Jady were of one mind about everything except their religions, and that topic they ignored when together. To al-Jady, Solomon and his fellow Jews were *dhimmi*, People of the Book, for like the Arabs, they were descendants of Abraham and worshiped his God. To Solomon, al-Jady was a friend worthy of respect, even though he was a follower of Mohammed. They could respect, if not accept, one another's religions because each claimed to worship one God and only one God.

More like brothers than most blood siblings, the two men treated each other's children like family and shared equally in the task of educating them.

"Examine your medicinal herbs regularly, once a week if possible," continued Solomon, using every possible moment for instruction. "And never apply a remedy you have not thoroughly tested."

"Yes, Father." Gavriel, too, had received similar instruction from Hakim al-Jady, but accepted repetition as part of the time-honored learning process.

The Jews' Inn was a tall, narrow building at the edge of Cordoba's Jewish quarter. Dank, stale air enveloped the three as they entered it. Three men sat idly in the front room. One of them, dressed in the striped, flowing garment of a Levantine Jew, wove nervous fingers together and gazed up at Solomon with hollow eyes. "I cannot pay," he said flatly. "I'm a stranger to Cordoba, and I have nowhere else to stay."

"Relax, friend, we are not here to collect payment," Solomon assured him. "All traveling Jews are welcome in this inn. We are here to visit the sick. Are you feeling well today?"

The man looked away. "My body is well enough,

but my heart is sick. They took everything, those Knights of the Cross. They killed my neighbors. They turned me out of my house, said they needed it for themselves."

Nizar clenched his teeth and shook his head in disgusted rage.

Solomon set a hand on the man's head and muttered a quick blessing from the Psalms. At that moment, Rabbi Maimon entered, leading his small son, Moses, by the hand.

His face awash with relief, Solomon announced, "Now here is our rabbi, come to comfort you." He kissed the rabbi's hand, as did Gavriel.

Maimon hurried to the Levantine Jew and sat opposite him, taking little Moses on his knee. Soon the boy, a curly-haired child with immense brown eyes, was chattering and bringing a smile to the stranger's careworn face.

"Are there any sick in this inn today?" asked Solomon.

One of the other men glanced up. "There is a small girl with a stomach ailment upstairs," he said. "and a man with a blackened hand who cries out in the night from pain."

Gavriel and Nizar followed Solomon up a narrow, creaking staircase. They found the girl lying on a woolen blanket, watched over by an older brother while their parents had gone on an errand. Solomon nodded at Nizar.

"Do you speak Arabic?" Nizar asked the girl's brother as he knelt by her side.

The boy nodded.

"How long has she suffered?"

"Since last evening."

"What did she eat yesterday?"

"Cracked wheat ... a little spiced mutton from the marketplace."

Nizar ran deft hands over the child's swollen abdomen. He laid an ear on the taut belly and tapped the skin with two knuckles. The child writhed and moaned. Nizar pried open her lips and smelt her breath. He pressed on her belly as if trying to make out the contours of her bowels.

At last he withdrew to consult with Solomon. "The meat she ate must have been rancid, Hakim. I have seen it all too often. Vendors disguise the taste of rotting meat with spices and sell it to the poor."

"A wise assumption. And what do you recommend?" asked Solomon.

"An infusion of ground ginger root and wormwood."

"Well done. Prepare and administer it."

Next it was Gavriel's turn. As they climbed a second narrow staircase, the specter of the blackened hand haunted him. Already he feared the diagnosis and its horrifying cure.

The patient, a man of middle age, lay curled up on his threadbare traveling mat, facing the wall. A nauseating stench permeated the room. At a nudge from his father, Gavriel approached and touched the fellow's shoulder. The suffering man groaned in agony. "T-tell me about your injury."

"It happened onboard ship," whispered the patient. "I caught my hand on a loose iron nail head.

The cut was small; I thought it had healed, but then my skin began to turn black. By the time we anchored at Cadiz, the whole hand was black and swollen."

Holding his breath, Gavriel ran tentative fingers along the hideous limb. The flesh was clearly dead, and oozing pus.

The patient continued, "I tried to wash it in hot oil, but it only grew worse. Now it gives off a terrible stench."

His throat filling with disgust, Gavriel grasped at his deepest reserves of willpower to keep from vomiting. He averted his eyes from the festering hand.

"Examine the hand, Gavriel," urged Nizar impatiently. He was like a young horse, fitted for a rider, pushing at a gate and eager to run, while Gavriel shrank from the bridle.

"You must inspect the diseased area more closely, Son," echoed Solomon.

Reluctantly Gavriel took the hand into his own. Sunlight streaming through a small window provided enough illumination to make a diagnosis. "It is the *Francorum ignis*," he pronounced in a ragged voice. *Gangrene.*

"And what do you recommend as treatment?"

"It must ... it must be ... " Waves of nausea crashed against Gavriel's insides. He took a deep breath and held it.

"It must be amputated!" exclaimed Nizar before Solomon could place a staying hand on his shoulder.

Gavriel felt the blood drain from his head. It

seemed to flow down through his body and seep into the scuffed wooden floor planking, leaving him as fragile as a dead leaf.

"No, please," begged the infected man. "I am a silversmith and need my two hands!"

"The wound's poison will kill you if the hand is not removed," reasoned Solomon. "It is a great loss, but not so great as loss of life."

Nizar had already removed a small, jagged saw from Solomon's satchel. Now he offered it to Gavriel.

"Please, Nizar," Gavriel rasped. "You do it."

Nizar looked at Solomon.

The hakim closed his eyes as if reckoning with deep disappointment. "Go ahead, Nizar."

As Nizar set to work, Gavriel dragged himself to a far corner of the room. Knees drawn up and head hanging between them, he wept in silent humiliation.

꽃 꽃 꽃

The following day, Hakim al-Jady accompanied both boys to the maristan, a low, sprawling building attached to a mosque. Many Muslims who could not afford to pay a private physician flocked to this place, where the doors were always open to them. As Solomon had done, al-Jady nudged each boy forward in his turn, hovering in the background, to ask questions and prompt them when they hesitated. Though the Arab hakim tried to be subtle about it, it was obvious to Gavriel that al-Jady entrusted to Nizar those patients with serious wounds or critical illnesses. To Gavriel he assigned the tasks of squeez-

ing garlic juice into an infected eye, wrapping a
sprained wrist and applying a salt and flour poultice
to a beesting – all ailments his mother could heal just
as easily with home remedies. Disgrace and humiliation dogged him throughout the day. In the evening,
as the two medical students washed hands in the
maristan courtyard, Nizar gave Gavriel a sympathetic smile.

"Don't worry," he said. "You're only fourteen. It
was hard for me, too, when I was that age."

Gavriel rolled his eyes. "Nizar, it has *never* been
hard for you. You were born to be a physician."

"And so were you."

"No, I wasn't."

"Yes, you *were*. You are a Zafrani. You are *the*
Zafrani of your generation. Are you going to let a bit
of stomach weakness keep you from fulfilling your
destiny? Allah made you an only son in the house of
a great healer. Will you really be so selfish as to toss
away that honor, just because you find it difficult to
face blood and ... and ... "

"Stop, Nizar."

But Nizar grabbed Gavriel by the shoulders and
shook him. "You must rise above it! Your mind must
master your stomach!"

"Boys!" Al-Jady came striding toward them, a
frown darkening his face. "Quiet down. You're dis-
turbing the patients."

Nizar let go, arching his eyebrows at Gavriel as
if to say, *It's up to you. You have a choice to make.*

Traversing a broad plaza on the way home,
al-Jady spoke of the patients seen that day, recount-

ing their symptoms, diagnoses and treatments. He discussed possible alternative remedies and was just launching into a lecture on bloodletting when a shout from a narrow side alley silenced him. A violent scuffle broke out at the doorway of a small adobe house. A horse reared. Suddenly a man broke loose from the mêlée. He raced up the alley toward al-Jady. The Almoravid soldier astride the horse kicked hard at the animal's flanks and pursued. Before al-Jady could leap to one side, the fugitive slammed into him, knocking him backward into the boys. All three tumbled to the ground just seconds before the great beast thundered past, hooves crashing against stone pavement. Sprawled on the ground, they watched the horseman raise a sword high above his head. Closing in on his barefoot quarry, he brought the glittering blade down in a swift, graceful arc. His victim dropped in the dust. For a moment, the plaza fell silent except for the horse's clopping and snorting. The rider slowed to a trot and circled back toward the fallen one. Whooping cheers rose from the alley. A small herd of green-turbaned, veiled men rushed from the door of the house toward the victim, shaking their fists and screaming curses.

If the man is not dead, thought Gavriel, *he soon will be.*

But the man lay motionless.

Astride the prancing Arabian, the swordsman exulted, hoisting the bloody blade in the air amid the cheers and shouts of his compatriots.

"Murderers!" screamed a woman. She stood alone in the alley, clutching a small child to her breast. Her hair was disheveled, a blue scarf slid down around her neck. "My husband did nothing wrong!"

One of the Almoravids turned back and marched toward her, wagging a reproachful finger. By the man's black clerical robes it was clear he was a _mullah_. "Your husband," he said, "was disloyal to the Prophet and the one true faith! Listen, people!" he shouted to the gathering crowd. "Any Muslim who marries a Christian or a Jew is a traitor to Mohammed."

The onlookers gasped and tensed as if expecting a blow. The haughty mullah strutted along the edge of the crowd, staring down his nose at each one he passed. "The days of the Caliphs are long past. After forty years of Almoravid rule, you Cordobans still have not learned to change your free and easy ways? We will _not_ tolerate Muslims mixing freely with Jews and Christians!"

"But are they not people of the book?" protested a man from the safety of the crowd.

"Yes, they are dhimmi," agreed the mullah as he scanned his audience with a suspicious eye. "And as such we allow them to practice their religions. But followers of Mohammed will no longer be suffered to marry or enter into business partnerships with them!"

Amid murmurs and sobs, the gathering disbanded. Al-Jady and the boys paused briefly beside the crumpled form lying in the plaza. The weeping woman, still clutching her child, sat beside her husband's body on the bloody pavement. The hakim knelt down and felt for a pulse. He found none.

"Return to your house now," al-Jady discreetly advised her. "There is nothing more to be done. I will send someone to carry him home."

Shaken, the boys followed the hakim back to the empty dispensary, where he sank onto a wooden stool. Slowly he began to unwind his turban.

"I have seen enough," he said, wiping sweat from his brow with the turban cloth. "We must leave Cordoba."

CHAPTER FIVE

But Father!" Nizar's face, already pale from the brutal scene he had witnessed, contorted with alarm.

"I have been thinking about this already for quite some time," the physician disclosed. "Gavriel, if your father has any sense, and I know better than anyone that he has much, he will leave Cordoba too."

Nizar thrust his face into his father's. "But this is our home! It has always been our home!"

Al-Jady reached up and touched his son's chin with trembling fingers. "How long will the Almoravids overlook a Jew and a Muslim practicing medicine together? Even if Solomon and I give up our partnership and practice separately, I am no longer willing to live under such an oppressive rule."

❧ ❧ ❧

That night al-Jady came alone after dark to the Zafrani house. He slipped off his sandals and sat down with the family around a platter of fresh fig slices sprinkled with sugar and cinnamon. Ever proper, he averted his eyes respectfully as Rohel greeted him. She instructed Mira to bring refreshment, and then left the men to themselves.

Solomon made small talk about the dispensary until Mira finished serving drinks and retired for the night. Finally he, al-Jady, Uncle Reuven, Nahum and Gavriel faced one another in solemn council.

"Your son has surely informed you of the scene he witnessed today," said al-Jady, sipping a cup of sweet mint tea.

Solomon nodded gravely. "And he has told me of your ... plans."

"I am not here, Solomon, to ask your permission to leave Cordoba," said the Muslim. "I have come, rather, to persuade you to leave also."

An audible gasp behind a curtained doorway confirmed what Gavriel already suspected – his mother was listening on the other side.

"I am grateful, Zahid, for your concern. How could I even begin to practice medicine without you, who are like a brother to me?"

"Yes, yes," agreed al-Jady with a wave of his hand, "we are like brothers. That is why ... "

"But as I was saying," Solomon interrupted, raising a hand, "neither I nor my wife could possibly imagine living anywhere other than Cordoba."

The Arab hakim wagged his head in dismay. "My brother, do you not see the ever-increasing danger around us? And those who know such things are saying it is only a matter of time until a new band of Berber fanatics advances on Marrakesh. The

Almohads ... "

"Didn't I tell you? Didn't I already warn you about the Almohads?" interrupted Reuven. He turned pleadingly to the Muslim physician. "Maybe *you* can talk sense into him, Hakim. To me, his little brother, he turns a deaf ear."

Al-Jady cast a reproachful look at his dear friend. "Solomon, will you wait to feel an Almoravid or an Almohad blade on your neck before you recognize the danger? Or will you leave Cordoba now, of your own accord, and travel in peace? Because I'm telling you, it *will* come to that."

A muffled sob drew Solomon's eyes to the tapestry hanging in the doorway. Sadly, he dropped his gaze into his cup of wine, appearing to contemplate his own reflection in the dark liquid. "Zahid, I must think and pray about these things. I cannot make a hasty decision. You know that our families – both Rohel's and mine – have lived in Cordoba for centuries."

"As have mine," said the Arab.

A tense silence settled on the five, but Reuven soon broke it with a loud clearing of his throat. "While you are thinking and praying, brother, present this idea to the Almighty – that Gavriel accompany me to the Rhinelands."

There came a loud, choking gasp from the doorway. The tapestry rustled. Rohel's slippers slap-slapped down the hallway as she fled. All eyes turned to Reuven.

He met them defiantly. "You all know Gavriel has no love of the medical profession! Why force him into it? Our family has produced enough physicians. You have plenty of daughters, Solomon; why not find a son-in-law so inclined?"

Nahum raised both hands defensively. "Not me! I'm studying to be a rabbi."

Gavriel's throat went dry. His chest tingled and his head seemed to float. Why had he not thought of this? Because he had not dared. And now here was Uncle Reuven, thinking the unthinkable, saying the unspeakable, and turning the world topsy-turvy by breaking all tradition.

Again Solomon stared into his winecup. Reuven turned to Gavriel and winked. Nahum looked at Gavriel in alarm while al-Jady appeared lost in his own thoughts. After a time, al-Jady came to himself and fixed his fellow physician with a solemn gaze. "Perhaps your brother is right, Solomon. Your son, clever as he is, seems to have little stomach for our profession."

Gavriel's pulse seemed to stop as he waited for a word from his father. But Solomon only sighed.

"Brother, face the truth!" Reuven pressed. "I can give the boy a chance to become a skilled trader. He will see the world! After the Rhinelands, he could accompany me to the Levant, to Egypt, even as far as Kai Feng Foo!"

"Al-Andalus is the very center of the civilized world," protested Solomon. "Why does he need to see other places?"

"Weren't you just telling us how dangerous the Levant is for a Jew?" Nahum challenged.

"Psssht!" Reuven dismissed the comment with

an irritated wave of his hand. "I know how to avoid trouble! I can get along just fine anywhere in the world."

Solomon looked up at Gavriel. "Would you willingly forfeit the calling to heal and the title of hakim in order to deal in silks and spices?"

"I *would*, Father."

Solomon bit his lip and blinked rapidly, clearly fighting back tears. An eternity seemed to pass before he whispered, "Then go with my blessing, if you must."

Gavriel jumped up and kissed his father's hand as the others looked on in astonishment. "Thank you, thank you!"

When Solomon had composed himself, he said sadly, "The question now is, after your sojourn to the Rhinelands, will you still have a home in Cordoba to return to? I must pray ... I must pray."

🙶 🙶 🙶

It seemed Gavriel was all Reuven had been waiting for in order to begin his journey. "You will be an invaluable help to me," he told the boy as Aziz loaded baggage onto a cart bound for the Guadalquivir River. "My own son is small and still needs his mother. And," he added, placing a firm hand on Gavriel's shoulder, "You have the makings of an excellent trader. I can see it in your eyes."

Perhaps, thought Gavriel hopefully. *But perhaps what Uncle Reuven sees is only my fear and excitement.* He had never before left Cordoba. Why should he have? His parents, sisters and two grandmothers lived here, and though his uncles and their families had spread themselves out from Fez to Seville, Granada and Marseilles, they all in turn came back to visit Cordoba. Despite the ruthless Almoravids, it had never occurred to Gavriel that he might one day leave the grand old city. Now here he was, crushed in the arms of his weeping mother, kissing his small sisters, facing his father, who though clearly disappointed, was putting on a gracious face for the occasion.

Gavriel wore a new tunic embroidered with indigo blue thread. From his shoulders hung a fur-trimmed mantle, not unlike Reuven's splendid garment, which Solomon had bought for him as a parting gift. Rohel's gift of a sleek leather shoulder bag held dried fruits, nuts, a pouch of silver dirhams, a double-edged knife and vials of medicinal herbs that Solomon insisted he take along. Attached to his belt was a brand new goatskin flask to hold drink. But what pleased him most were the stylish leather boots Reuven had brought him from Fez and had managed to keep concealed until now. They were soled with leather rather than the usual cork, reaching to the middle of his calves with laces up the sides. True travelers' boots, these were made to endure and protect feet in all climates.

Rohel turned back inside, taking comfort in her daughters' embraces. Solomon accompanied Reuven and Gavriel to the quay, where an Arab _dhow_ waited to carry them downriver to Cadiz. Reuven, seeing Solomon eye the old-fashioned teakwood vessel with its strange, triangular sails, laid a reassuring hand on his elder brother's arm. "Have no fear, Solomon. Your son is in good hands; he has a glorious future ahead of him."

"Gavriel!" Nizar al-Jady came striding down the quay with a bundle in his hands. His father followed closely behind. "Gavriel, I've brought you – –"

Al-Jady seized his son by the shoulder, pulling him to an abrupt halt. A veiled horseman in white robes and green turban was advancing toward them. Nizar backed up closer to his father.

"What is your business with these Jews?" barked the soldier through the folds of his veil.

Al-Jady said something Gavriel could not quite hear. Waiting anxiously, he glanced up and down the quay and noticed more armed Almoravids patrolling the crowded waterfront.

"So, it has come to this," muttered Uncle Reuven under his breath.

The horseman trotted his mount off to one side, but turned in the saddle to watch what the al-Jadys would do. Clutching the bundle to his chest, Nizar gave Gavriel a defeated farewell look. Al-Jady put an arm around his son's shoulders and led him away, glancing sorrowfully backward. Gavriel watched until they disappeared into the crowd.

"Describe again to me your route," said Solomon, attempting to divert attention from the unfortunate incident.

"We sail to Cadiz," replied Reuven, holding up one finger after another, "and then to Marseilles ... up the Rhône to Lyon, proceeding northeast to the Rhine, and then across it, into the Rhinelands."

"So far!" exclaimed Solomon, barely able to choke out the words. For a few awkward moments he struggled to compose himself. He clasped Reuven's arm in farewell. "Give my warmest greetings to Baruch." He embraced his son one last time before turning abruptly away. The physician hurried up the quay and disappeared into a narrow lane. Gavriel moved as if to run after his father, but Reuven stopped him. "Let him go. This is his way of saying good bye without weeping in public."

With a painful lump rising in his throat, Gavriel boarded the dhow and aimed a last look at Cordoba. As the boat rocked heavily on the swollen river, he bid silent farewell to familiar landmarks - the Great Mosque, perched fortress-like on a hill, its minaret clawing at the sky ... the immense, creaking water-wheel, turning river water aside into fields to water crops ... the boulevards lined with swaying palms.

Another soldier walked his horse along the waterfront. The Almoravid's dark, narrowed eyes stared hard at Gavriel as if warning, "Be careful, dhimmi, what you do and say. You are not out of Cordoba yet!"

సౌ సౌ సౌ

Two days sailing downriver brought them to Cadiz, which shimmered like a giant pearl set on a sapphire bay. Its waters teemed with boats and rang with the shouts of fishermen casting their nets. Reuven, Gavriel and Aziz found lodging in a respectable inn until Reuven's goods could be reclaimed and passage booked on a boat bound for Marseilles. They found an old but seaworthy cog, piloted by a cranky Mozarab with a bald, sunburned head. Since Reuven refused to load his goods and entrust them to the Christian crew, he left Aziz to spend the final night on board before the morning's departure. Hurrying back to the inn, Reuven led Gavriel through the heart of the city. He knew exactly where to turn, moving with ease and confidence through the winding lanes and alleys.

"We have found an excellent ship," he exulted, pulling his nephew to one side as a heavy-laden donkey clopped past. "Its captain seems a capable and reasonably honest man. I tell you, one can never take such things for granted...."

Suddenly two figures emerged from a shadowed doorway. They darted straight at Reuven. Gavriel saw the flash of a blade in a quick hand.

"What have you got for us, Jew?" growled the one with the knife. He shoved Reuven up against a stone wall. His companion caught Gavriel by one arm and twisted it. "Show us what you're carrying!"

A wrenching pain shot through Gavriel's elbow. His eyes blurred. Like a sickly lamb he bleated out a pathetic "Help!" but there was no one to hear him. The alley was empty. Reuven shouted something, but the blood pounding in Gavriel's head obscured it. Another hard shove, and Gavriel's head slammed against stone. He felt himself sinking. The wall now loomed where the sky should be, but a sudden hand caught hold of him and pulled him up. It was Reuven. He had unloosed a leather pouch from around his neck and tossed it on the ground, scattering coins. As the thieves scrambled after them, he dragged his nephew back down to the mouth of the alley toward a crowded street.

Behind the stall of a crockery seller, the two clung together and caught their breaths. It had all happened so fast! Reuven inspected his nephew's head. "It's only a bad bruise," he said, but Gavriel could already feel it swelling into a large lump.

"Uncle, they took your money!" he gasped,

shaking uncontrollably.

Reuven's eyes darted back toward the alley. "No, they didn't. They stole only a tiny purse I carry for just such occasions. At the most I keep a mere ten dirhams in it." Trying to appear casual, he ran his fingers across his midsection, feeling reassuringly the astrolabe's contours. He took Gavriel's hand and brushed it against a small bump beneath his cloak sleeve, attached to his arm. "Here is the real money pouch – the one we cannot afford to lose."

Gavriel squeezed his uncle's hand. "We're all right, then? We're all right?"

"Yes," Reuven replied, "but this is a timely reminder. We must take every precaution from this day forward."

And so it was that Reuven hurried to a clothing shop and bought Gavriel a new set of garments. In the morning, the trader removed his gold necklace and all his rings and from deep in his own travel bag retrieved a white _burnoose_ and green turban cloth, identical to the ones he had bought his nephew. "I did not think we would need these while still in Sefarad," he confessed as he removed his elegant cloak and pulled the loose Arab garment over his head. He motioned for Gavriel to do the same.

Gavriel hesitated.

"Put it on, boy!" Reuven ordered. "For as long as we need to be, you and I are Berber Almoravids. How lucky for us they veil their faces!"

Reluctantly, Gavriel donned the burnoose. He forced himself to stand still while his uncle expertly wound the green cloth around his head and tucked the end neatly under the folds. Feeling uneasy all the way down to the harbor, the boy avoided all eyes, as if each passerby could see through the veil and discover he was a Jew playing at masquerade. Once, Gavriel had pretended to be Haman at a Purim celebration. He had costumed himself like the vile man by winding one of his mother's silk scarves around his head and staining his chin with ashes to make a beard. But this disguise felt more wicked than portraying that long ago enemy of Jews. Taking on the appearance of a Mohammedan! To live near, to respect, and to work alongside the people of that false religion was one thing. To exchange gifts with them at Purim and Ramadan, to laugh and feast with them was one thing – to pretend to *be* one was another matter entirely. Would the Holy One over-look this offense? Reuven assured him that he had secured permission from his rabbi in Fez, but who was that rabbi to Gavriel? If only he had known, he would have asked permission of Rabbi ben Maimon in Cordoba! Now it was too late.

༒ ༒ ༒

Under the bald captain's expert guidance, the cog hoisted anchor right on schedule and departed for Marseilles. It wasn't until Gavriel saw the coast of Sefarad recede into a shimmering haze that he began to feel the first wretched pangs of seasickness. He leaned over the gunwale and vomited until he was dizzy and weak. His head still throbbed from the robber's blow.

"Uncle, is the Almighty punishing me?" he gasped.

Reuven laughed. "For what? Leaving home?"

"For dressing as a Muslim!"

Clapping a reassuring hand on the boy's back, Reuven said, "Gavriel, the Holy One is not without a sense of humor. He who knows all sees beneath the clothing and knows your heart is Jewish. As for your seasickness, it may comfort you to know that *I* no longer feel the waves, though I used to feel them – every bit as much as you – when I first began traveling."

Gavriel slipped his travel bag off his shoulder and let it drop at Reuven's feet. "Open it, Uncle," he instructed, holding tight to the rail to keep from toppling. "There is a vial of ginger root powder inside. Drop a little on my tongue, and then give me water."

Reuven followed his nephew's instructions. Eventually Gavriel's stomach calmed enough to let him eat a little matzoh.

CHAPTER SIX

CHAPTER VI

Reuven appeared equally at home in the
Frankish port of Marseilles as in Cordoba and Cadiz.
He hailed a carter and pressed a few silver deniers
in the man's callous palm. "To the home of Baruch
Zafrani," he said, "in the Jewish quarter!"

Uncle Baruch's house rose imposingly above a
palm-lined boulevard. Built of pale, polished stone, its
façade glowed red where bathed in the early morning sun. It was a fashionable neighborhood; men in
black silk caftans and yellow, pointed hats strolled
past, pausing to converse beneath shady palm fronds.
Reuven clanged a bronze doorknocker shaped like
a lion's head. Soon a girl with loosely braided hair
peered down from a window. A look of terror dis-
torted her face.

"Shifra, it's me!" Reuven pulled the veil from his
face.

Shifra broke into a slow, comprehending smile
and disappeared from the window. When the door
swung wide, the girl darted in front of the surprised
Slav who had opened it, embracing the uncle she

obviously knew well.

"Peace be to you, dear Niece," said Reuven, kissing her hand.

"And to you a goodly blessing, Uncle," she properly responded.

"I've brought a surprise!" Reuven pushed Gavriel forward. "Your cousin from Cordoba."

"Not uncle Solomon's boy!" Shifra exclaimed. Her hazel eyes devoured Gavriel's eyes and nose with hungry curiosity. He unwrapped his veil and smiled down at her. No more than sixteen, she resembled an impish princess, bedecked in silver bracelets and gold earrings. The same narrow, dark features that ran through all the Zafranis defined her face.

"Zelenka" she commanded the Slav in the woman's own language, "bring warm lavender water for my uncle and cousin to wash with."

The slave, much younger than Mira, yet possessing the same round, ruddy face and narrow eyes, bowed slightly and disappeared into the depths of the house.

"She's new," said Shifra matter-of-factly. "She knows not one word of Frankish or Hebrew yet."

"What happened to Dobrila?" Reuven asked.

"She died."

"May she rest," murmured uncle and nephew in unison.

Small Shifra looked up at them in surprise. "Dobrila was a Christian," she said, as if that would dispel any notion of a peaceful afterlife. The girl shot an imperious glance at Aziz, who stood aloof near the front gate beside a mound of baggage.

Gavriel bit back a smile. He had always heard stories of how Uncle Baruch, a man with no sons, raised his eldest daughter as if she were a boy. Word had it that he educated her in Torah and Talmud and carried on lively discussions with her at the supper table. Clearly, this lordly girl thought herself equal to any man, for instead of allowing Reuven to take care of matters, she looked Aziz directly in the eye and ordered him to bring Baruch's goods into the house at once.

Unfazed, Reuven asked, "But where is your father? Still asleep, perhaps? Have I been lucky enough to catch him at home in Marseilles?"

"You *are* in luck, Uncle," she replied. "Five days ago he returned from Bohemia with a cargo of thirty Slavs. He's selling them today, down at the slave market."

Reuven's eyes lit up. "At the slave market, is he? Then Gavriel and I will hurry there and surprise him!"

Without asking whether her company was desired, Shifra draped a delicate scarf over her face, leaving only her left eye exposed, and set out with them into the city. Nestled at the foot of rugged hills, Marseilles sprawled down to the shore's edge. Gavriel's ears caught snatches of Arabic, Latin and Frankish in the streets. The crowds were so thick and moved so swiftly, the Zafranis had to fight to stay together. The three jostled their way through immense seafood and pottery markets before reaching the plaza where slaves were bought and sold.

A throng of men gathered around a raised platform. The silky black of Jews, the bleached white of Muslims and the colored tunics of Frankish Christians mingled as the customers crowded together, straining to see over shoulders and heads in order to evaluate the merchandise. A handful of Venetian merchants stood out in the crowd, attired in exquisite fabrics and long, pointed shoes.

"We have young, strong men and women of the Slavonic race!" barked an Arab dealer in a purple turban. An immense pearl clung to a ring on his finger, so large it resembled a pigeon's egg. The Arab pointed out the thick neck and broad shoulders of the captive standing beside him. The slave, like most of his people, was squarely built, with enough muscle to make up for what he lacked in height. "This one will relieve you of the burden of carrying your daily water from the well! Do you deal in trade, with goods to transport? This one will do the heavy lifting and spare your back!"

A few unenthusiastic bids drifted up from the crowd. No one seemed anxious to purchase a slave so quickly, not when twenty-nine more still waited, off to one side of the platform. Dazed and disoriented, the Slavs slumped in the shade along the wall of a church, linked together by a rope that circled twice around each waist. Their hands were bound with hemp.

A stately, bearded Jew loosed a young woman and led her up the platform steps. Immediately Gavriel recognized his uncle.

"Ah, my friends, I see you are all thinking over

very carefully any purchases you might make," he shouted. "Very wise, very wise. Think as much as you like, for we have thirty Slavs to choose from today, fresh from the forests of Bohemia!"

Reuven, Gavriel and Shifra watched the spectacle with interest until only a handful of captives remained. Finally the Arab dealer waved away the crowd, proclaiming that the buying and selling were finished for the day. The unsold Slavs huddled closely together, eyes darting about uncertainly.

When the crowd had thinned, Reuven approached Baruch and tapped his shoulder from behind. "Congratulations, Brother. I see you have done a brisk business today."

Baruch spun around and grasped his youngest brother in a fierce embrace. "And you – you sly trader," he growled playfully, "what schemes do you have up your sleeve these days?"

For the second time that day, Reuven pushed Gavriel forward. "None other than Solomon's son, Gavriel."

Baruch stared in wonder at the boy. "Can it be? All the way from Cordoba, may God protect it. How you've changed since the last time I saw you! But I shouldn't wonder at that. You must be a practicing physician by now."

Gavriel licked nervous lips. He dreaded seeing disappointment on this face that so resembled his father's. "I *was* to be a physician. But it has been decided that I'm better suited to a trader's life."

Answering only with raised eyebrows, Baruch studied his nephew's face. "That comes as a great surprise to me. Tell me, is your father pleased at your choice of livelihood?"

Gavriel looked away.

Reuven rescued him. "Solomon has accepted it. The boy's not cut out to be a physician."

Baruch considered this a moment with an undisguised look of doubt. Then with a wave of his hand he dismissed the subject and put an arm around each of them. "For as long as you like, you will both make my home yours."

"Your daughter," said Reuven, "has already made us welcome."

"Ah, Shifra," laughed Baruch, catching sight of the girl, who had approached the frightened Slavs and was even now speaking to them in their tongue. He raised his hands skyward in a dramatic, helpless gesture. "What kind of riddle are we Zafranis? A family of brothers who beget mostly girls! It must be the Almighty's little joke."

"Ah yes, but she's a clever girl!" laughed Reuven.

"She is indeed. If I could, I would send her along with you to learn the art of trading; she has the kind of sharp, keen mind that is perfect for it. Yet what choice do I have but to marry her off, and soon?"

Reuven glanced at the diminutive girl across the plaza. "Yes, I see what you mean. When will she marry?"

"Before the year is out, to the son of a well-respected Marseillaise family. Still, it rankles me. To have a boy to carry on after me ... of this I can only dream." He turned to Gavriel. "I can well imagine how Solomon must feel at seeing you fly away."

Gavriel shifted uncomfortably in his new boots. Again, he glanced at the remaining slaves - a middle-aged woman, a too-thin girl with scabs on her face, and the bull-necked man who had stood on the block when he first arrived. All too aware that he was a disappointment, he abruptly changed the subject. "And what about those?" he asked with a nod toward the three. "What happens to them?"

Baruch shrugged. "I will sell them eventually. For now, I take them home. Come, let's hurry."

ॐ ॐ ॐ

Baruch's home, like Solomon's, was filled with elegant furnishings and plush carpets. With the help of no less than four house slaves, Baruch's wife spread a fabulous meal before her guests. The family feasted joyfully. In Marseilles as in Cordoba, Reuven became the center of his relatives' attention, captivating them with amusing stories and dramatic gestures.

Long after her mother and younger sisters retired to their rooms, Shifra continued dipping her bread into a savory garlic sauce. Though the hour was late, she showed no sign whatsoever of modestly withdrawing from the men's conversation.

"How much did you get from the highest bidder today, Father?" she brazenly inquired.

Baruch was unoffended. "Three hundred and sixty deniers. That was for the tallest youth, the one with the long arms."

"And how much money did you make altogether?"

"I haven't counted yet. It's complicated; I was paid in dirhams *and* deniers. There are even a few Venetian ducats mixed in. I'll do the reckoning another day."

"I'll do it for you," she offered, chewing the meat off an olive and spitting the pit into a bowl. Shifra turned to Reuven. "And you, Uncle Reuven? What are you dealing in these days?"

Her boldness shocked Gavriel. His sister Ashira would never dream of sitting as the only female among men, spitting olive pits into a dish and asking them questions about their business.

But, like his brother, Reuven seemed unfazed by her manner. "Perfumes, a few medicinals, silks and spices ... the usual. *And* something special." He reached beneath his caftan and gently extracted the precious astrolabe.

Shifra took it into her delicate hands with the care one might give a newborn child. "Ah! Look at it," she cooed. "The engraving on the plates is so intricate! And the framework is exceptionally sturdy. It will fetch you a mighty price."

"Indeed it will. A Rhineland bishop has already spoken for it."

Baruch sighed and sipped a cool drink made of grape syrup. "Your cargo is easier than mine. You don't have to feed or clothe it."

"Perhaps not," replied Reuven, "but I'm constantly on guard against thieves. Who would steal a Slav?"

Before going to bed, Gavriel wandered out to the courtyard. A gentle sea wind stirred in the fronds of the palms encircling the fountain. He dipped his

fingers in the cool, gurgling water. In a few moments
he heard the tinkling of ankle bracelets behind him.
Shifra seated herself on the fountain's edge.

"I've heard you're a scholar," said Gavriel.

She flashed a proud smile. "I've studied Torah
and Talmud since I lost my first baby tooth."

Shifra drew up her knees and encircled them
with her arms. With her long gown bunched up
around her feet, she looked like one of Reuven's
bundles of silk. "Tell me, Cousin Gavriel, are you
really going to abandon your physician's training to
become a trader?"

Though her eyes were obscured in shadow he
could feel them piercing into him. He decided to
meet her question with courage. "I mean to, absolutely! The fact is that I have no stomach for blood
and such."

She shook her head in disbelief. "Do you know
how much I long to follow in my grandfather's footsteps and learn the art of healing? The human body
and the diagnosing of disease fascinate me! But even
if I studied medicine, as a girl I would never be allowed to practice it."

Struck by the absurd thought of a woman practicing medicine, Gavriel began to chuckle.

"Why are you laughing? It makes perfect sense.
Do you treat women in your dispensary?"

"Rarely," he admitted. "Only if a woman's husband or father comes along and gives permission."

"You see! Is the thought of a female physician
treating other women so preposterous then?"

Shifra had a point. Although wealthy women

availed themselves of the finest medical care, poor women, especially Muslims, were left to the devices of relatives bumbling along with home remedies. Yet Gavriel simply could not imagine there ever coming a day when a female would be trained as a physician. He offered his cousin what he hoped was a reassuring smile. "I heard you're getting married soon. I can teach you a few herbal remedies so you can care for your children when they're ill."

She rolled her eyes and turned away. "You are just like the rest of them."

"I'm sorry. My fifteen-year-old sister, Ashira, is married already. She was happy to marry."

"Well *my* life has been different from Ashira's" she retorted. "*I* am different! I've read Aristotle, Galen and Hippocrates. I've studied logic, mathematics and astronomy, yet now I'm expected to lay aside everything I've learned and be content to manage a household. It's not that I don't want to marry and have children. I *do* want those things. I like being a girl – yet I can't help but wonder sometimes what good I might have accomplished in the world, if only I had been born a boy!"

Horrified, Gavriel put a finger to his lips to silence her. "Shifra, it isn't wise to question the Almighty like that. He made you a girl, and that is his plan for you."

"And you?" she retorted. "Didn't you question the Almighty when you threw away your medical training and decided to become a trader?"

"That's different!"

She gave him a long, hard look. "It's only different because you are a boy and have the freedom to do the things you want."

Now it was Gavriel's turn to shake his head in disbelief. How odd it sounded for a female to talk like this! It had never occurred to him that a girl could crave knowledge beyond the confines of her home and the women's gallery in the synagogue. He wondered whether Uncle Baruch hadn't made a grave mistake in educating Shifra. Where might such a thing lead? *What should I do?* he thought. Should he leave her sitting here and tomorrow pretend she had never revealed such scandalous thoughts to him? He cast about in his mind for something comforting to say.

"Maybe you'll enjoy running a household."

She did not answer, and a long silence followed. A loud snore startled Gavriel. The sound of a woman's weeping momentarily rose above the gurgling of the fountain. Shifra gestured toward a locked, windowless room across the courtyard. "The Slavs sleep in there," she explained. "It's where Father keeps them until buyers are found. Don't worry. They have enough to eat and drink. They have blankets to lie on."

Just as Gavriel was on the verge of saying goodnight, Shifra whispered, "Gavriel, don't think I am not eager to marry and have a family. It will be a joy for me to teach my children the things I have learned. But remember me when you are traveling and buying and selling. Remember how I would give anything to have the honor of healing the sick, and how I cannot – *ever* – just because I am a girl."

83

That night Gavriel thanked God that he had been born a male. He thought of the sickening smells in the dispensary and closed his eyes and imagined himself in the Rhinelands, cutting business deals with bishops and abbots and rich merchants. His father had given his all-important consent. Nothing would hold him back. The world lay before him and his destiny was his to decide.

CHAPTER SEVEN

Chapter VII

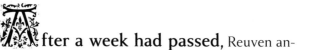

After a week had passed, Reuven announced that it was time to set out again. Only hours before boarding a barge bound for Lyon, he decided to trade Aziz for one of Baruch's leftover Slavs. He chose the bull-necked, muscular man for whom no one had bid high enough to suit the dealers. Perhaps the fellow had remained unsold because he looked strong enough to break the ropes that bound him and frightened enough to bolt. But none of this deterred Reuven.

"He calls himself Damek," Baruch explained. "He says he comes from a good family in a village near a great river, but what is that to you? Just call him whatever you like; he will get used to it."

Reuven decided to call him by his original name. Before setting out for the waterfront, he inspected the Slav's teeth and parted his shaggy hair to check for lice. When the man's scalp was found to be crawling with vermin, Reuven ordered his head shaved, then and there.

"I cannot take Aziz with me on the next leg

of my journey," Reuven informed Gavriel. "He's an excellent servant, but as you will one day learn, it's dangerous to take a Mohammedan into Christian lands. Being a Jew is dangerous enough, but to parade an infidel through France and the Rhinelands is asking for trouble! The sight of this bulky Slav will cause people to think twice before bothering us." He turned to his brother. "Tell him this, Baruch: if he sticks by Gavriel and me and protects us and steals nothing, I will pay him handsomely and grant him his freedom when we return to al-Andalus."

Baruch translated Reuven's message for the slave. The captive, whose shorn hair lay in ragged piles around his feet, nodded wary assent.

And so it was decided. Baruch and his family seemed glad to absorb the faithful Aziz into their home. What Aziz thought of this transaction, Gavriel could only guess. As his fate was haggled over, the man from al-Maghrib stood silently by with only the merest twitch of his jaw. He met no one's eyes.

Soon Aziz stood with Baruch and Shifra on the dock, watching his former master sail away. His arms were folded across his chest, like a shield against life and its unpredictable changes. He stood a little behind his new owners, head slightly bent as if waiting for their next command, looking as if he had always belonged to them and was accustomed to obeying their every wish.

As Gavriel watched Shifra's petite form shrink on the receding quay, he thought how the Cordoban grandmother they shared would be scandalized at the behavior of this forward girl. He felt sorry for

Shifra, sorry that her father had recklessly opened her mind when he ought to have kept it shut. There was no place in this world for an educated girl, after all.

On the deck of the barge, the newly shorn Damek perched atop Reuven's piled up cargo, which had been covered with oilcloth to protect it from the weather. He looked like a frightened, caged animal. Surrounded by the incomprehensible shouts of the Frankish crew, the Slav watched the dazzling port of Marseilles slip away. His gray eyes darted to and fro, taking in the endless expanse of fields on either side of the river. Either he could not swim or Reuven's promise had gained his faith, for he made no move to jump overboard and flee.

How good it felt to shed the Muslim clothing and dress as Jews again! The barge was laden with sugar cane, olives, oil and wine. Northward it sailed, past rocky, sun-bleached cliffs dotted with scraggly pines, blown along by a breeze laced with the scent of wild thyme. Crumbling remains of Roman villas dotted the countryside, forced to share their domain with newer farmhouses. Once Damek climbed down from his perch and tapped Reuven on the arm. He pointed at a certain tree and jabbered urgently in his unintelligible language. Was he imparting some bit of knowledge, or expressing astonishment at the un-familiar? When Reuven and Gavriel shrugged help-lessly, the slave shook his head in mute frustration.

"Oh, these newly captured Slavs," muttered Reuven. "They really do not know their place."

The journey took three weeks, during which the

Frankish sailors expertly guided the barge through the Rhône's shallows and wild currents. During the voyage, Reuven spent countless hours instructing Gavriel in Frankish, teaching him such rudimentary phrases as "My name is Gavriel" and "How much does this cost?" "The more languages a trader can speak, the better his chances of avoiding trouble and doing a brisk business," Reuven insisted. "We will concentrate on Frankish for now. Next comes Latin."

Uncle and nephew disembarked at Lyon, where Reuven promptly bought five pack mules with saddles. Together he and Gavriel slung their baggage onto the animals' backs and used hemp rope to fasten each mule's halter to the saddle of the mule in front.

It was early June now, the weather mild and changing every few days from sun to gentle rain. North of Lyon, the countryside gradually took on a lush appearance, with rich brown soil unlike the rocky terrain near the Mediterranean Sea. The sun here was soft and caressing, not harsh and blinding as in Spain. Stone villas became sparse, replaced with wooden, thatch-roofed barns, some of them round like beehives. Greenery ran wild here, helped along by the rains. The Roman road through thick forest would have been lonely and fraught with danger were it not for the Jews' new traveling companions – a pair of well-armed Swedes named Tarn and Sigurd. After venturing south with amber and the pelts of marten and beaver, these Northern traders were now returning home with wine, sugar and spices. They were tall and sinewy, each with a long sword at his side. By the act of tethering their own mules to Reuven's train, they signaled their willingness to share equally the hardships of the journey, thus making it less burdensome for all.

"Are they heathens?" Gavriel had whispered to his uncle as he watched Sigurd wrestling with the mules' tack before setting out.

"Probably not," Reuven replied. "Most Northmen have long since converted to Christianity. That *could* pose a problem for us."

But traveling with Jews seemed to bother Tarn and Sigurd not one bit. In fact, the Swedes' religion appeared to be a curious blend of Christianity and the pagan worship they had supposedly forsaken. Both men made the sign of the cross every night before lying down to sleep. But one June evening, after making camp in a small clearing, Tarn caught a squirrel, slit its throat, and suspended it from a pole he'd fashioned out of a fir branch and erected beside the campfire.

"Why aren't you eating it?" Reuven asked him.

Through hand signs, broken Frankish and snatches of Arabic learned on trade routes, the Northman made it clear that this was a sacrifice in honor of the god Thor. "Because sun in sky long this day."

"Ah, the summer solstice," said Reuven. "Of course."

Sigurd, who wore a silver cross around his neck, wove a crude garland of spruce and placed it on the ground beneath the gruesome sacrifice.

Both Northmen treated the Jews with courtesy

but looked with undisguised disdain upon the slave
Damek. "Slavs!" Sigurd growled once, making a gesture like the thrust of a knife. He turned aside and
spat contemptuously onto the ground. Yet having
had the satisfaction of thus expressing his disgust, he
never again threatened Damek. Reuven ignored the
outburst, and it was soon forgotten.

Tarn and Sigurd always tramped at the head of
the mule train, jabbering between themselves in their
bizarre, singsong tongue. They cut odd figures with
their wild, red-gold hair and full breeches gathered
at the knee. But each night as he fell asleep to the
sound of a crackling fire, owl hoots and wind moaning in the spruce trees, Gavriel thanked God for the
Swedes' comforting presence.

The land of the Franks appeared well cultivated
and bursting with grain. Along the edges of barley
and rye fields sprang delicate blooms of pink, yellow
and violet, utterly unlike the hardy wildflowers of
al-Andalus. Gone were the citrus groves and date
palms of his homeland. Because he had never traveled, it had never occurred to Gavriel that some
climates might nurture certain types of trees and
flowers while being hostile to others. He had considered himself well educated, having studied science
and geography along with a host of other subjects.
Yet now here he was, a babe filled with wonder, eyes
gradually opening onto the wider world.

The party of traders tramped steadily northward, following the River Saône. Gavriel began to
miss the roasted chicken, pilah, dates and olives of
al-Andalus. In these Frankish lands, whether he slept

in a monastery hostel or camped in the open, his diet consisted of coarse bread made of rye or spelt, smelly cheese, vegetable pottage and salted meat. The dried provisions from Cordoba had run out. Reuven bought food whenever they passed through a village, and to Gavriel's disgust he learned that his uncle was willing to lay aside Jewish law and eat rabbit or pork when threatened with hunger.

"I throw myself upon the mercy of the Almighty," Reuven boldly stated. "If a Jew is to survive, a Jew must at times step out of his Jewish skin."

In a village called Charnay, one day the travelers halted to buy food. While the Swedes visited a baker's stall, Reuven and Gavriel helped Damek water the mules at a public well. The last mule had just begun to drink when a rumbling sounded. Horses approached, shaking the ground with heavy hoofbeats. These animals, unlike the sleek, slender Arabians of the Almoravids, were thick-chested and stout-rumped.

"Ho there!" someone shouted.

"Whoa! Stop there!"

Suddenly surrounded by massive, snorting beasts, the pack mules backed into one another, tangling harnesses and jostling baggage. One brayed with a toothy grimace. Gavriel and Damek grabbed two mules' halters each, trying to steady them.

A man barked something in Frankish. Though Gavriel could not understand the foreign tongue, he knew by Reuven's expression that trouble brewed. Reuven pretended not to understand, but the Frank surprised him by switching to a clumsy Arabic. "I *asked*, what are Jews doing watering their animals at a Christian well, in a Christian town?"

Gavriel forced himself to look up, shielding his eyes from the sun. The man who glared down at him looked to be about thirty. His fleshy neck and cheeks were flushed red. His broad forehead glistened with sweat. Apparently well fed on the pork and cabbage and cheese of these parts, he grunted as he shifted his great bulk on the saddle. He wore a linen surcoat, open in front to reveal a dingy tunic that had once been white. Down the center of the tunic ran the faint outline of a cross. Faded pink lines traced the path of stitches that had once held it in place.

"Isn't it obvious what they're doing, Garin?" tossed off another of the knights in Frankish. This one looked equally road-weary, but with leaner build and indifferent expression. "Don't bother with them; just tell them to move."

"Bernard is right, Garin," said a pale young fellow whose hair hung to his shoulders. "Better do what he says."

Reuven prodded the last mule back toward the water bucket. "We'll be finished soon enough," he said with forced calm. "Only this last one left to go."

What happened next shocked even the other knights. Garin's face flamed. "Get away from this well!" he snarled, like a dog ready to tear flesh. "An *abbot* is coming to water his horse!" He moved his hand to the hilt of his sword and swung a leg over his saddle to dismount.

"Garin, watch yourself!" cautioned the pale one.

Damek backed up against the well.

93

"Please, Sir," said Reuven, "we are poor travelers, trying to make a living."

Garin guffawed loudly, pointing at Reuven's dusty but still-splendid cloak. "Poor travelers, eh? I know a rich Jew when I see one! I spent ten years in the Holy Land and I've seen plenty of Jews and Mohammedans in my day."

Eyes darting to the town's edge, Reuven whispered, "Run, Gavriel."

But Gavriel balked. Run where? This land was completely foreign to him. If he fled and was captured, might not he suffer a worse fate? He dropped the mules' halters, inched toward his uncle's side and stuck close.

"Filthy Jews," spat Garin as if he had just chewed a bitter nut. He slid heavily down from the saddle. Up close, his tunic was greasy and soaked with sweat. The steely grate of sword leaving scabbard raised gooseflesh on Gavriel's neck.

"We are Jews, it is true," admitted Reuven, holding up both hands. "But we are on a *bishop's* errand!"

Garin smirked.

"Better to leave these Jews alone," warned the long-haired youth. "His grace is coming!"

Ignoring the advice, Garin took a step forward. A sour wine stench blew out on his breath as he growled, "I'll teach you both a lesson you'll never forget, Christ killers!"

He hoisted his long sword and pressed it first against Gavriel's neck, then Reuven's. He held it there.

"Didn't you hear us?" hissed Bernard.

A second flurry of horses with riders clopped up
and surrounded the well.

"Look, Jews!" someone called out sportingly.
At the sight of Reuven and Gavriel held hostage by
Garin's sword, several broke into laughter.

"What's going on, men? What is it?"

Horses parted to let the speaker pass. Slender
and serious of expression, he wore a gray silk cloak
and white riding gloves. His hair was only beginning
to gray. When he lifted a hand to point at Garin, a
sapphire ring, fitted over the glove, sparkled in the
sun. "What *are* you doing?"

The man's voice worked like a potion on the
enraged Garin. The knight's pudgy hands trembled,
then relaxed and lowered the sword. "Just making
sure these Jews get their mules out of your horses'
way, Your Grace."

The abbot snorted with disgust at their behavior. "Good heavens, fellow, did you need to pick
a fight over that? We can wait our turn like anyone
else. When I hired an armed escort I didn't mean to
surround myself with childish bullies!"

Garin rolled his eyes and mouthed something
mockingly. He turned to face the abbot. "Beg pardon,
Your Grace."

"Nevermind. Let these men finish their water-
ing, and then take care of your horses." The abbot
dismounted. "Please forgive these churlish fellows.
It isn't safe to be a Jew these days, and I fear my
Heavenly Father is grieved by what a few misguided
Christians are doing in his name."

Reuven took the churchman's gloved hand and

gave it a respectful kiss. As he did so, his eyes lingered on the sapphire ring beneath his nose.

"May the Lord bless you and lend his mercy to your journey," said the abbot. Then he left the dusty street and entered the town inn to find refreshment.

Shaken but composed, Reuven ordered Damek to proceed with the watering. As the abbot's party withdrew several paces to wait, he muttered in Hebrew, "*Why* didn't I see this coming? I became too confident, that's why. From now on, Gavriel, we dress as Christians!"

"What?"

"You heard me correctly. The problem is, I have only one monk's habit. We'll make do somehow. Don't worry."

Still trembling, Gavriel kept a wary eye on the noisy cluster of knights. Perhaps his uncle was right and a Jew must do whatever it took to survive. Yet even so, the thought of disguising himself as a Christian disturbed him far more than wearing the garb of a Mohammedan. Christians, with their worship of Christ! How could a Jew, who prayed three times a day, *Hear oh Israel, the Lord our God, the Lord is One!* disguise himself as one of these?

When they were safely encamped to the north of Charnay, Reuven searched through the baggage until he located a brown woolen monk's habit. For Gavriel he found a simple russet tunic and belted it at the waist with a length of rope. "Aha, the final touch," he said, extracting a crucifix carved of olive-wood, suspended from a leather cord. He slipped it over Gavriel's head.

"This is going too far!" the boy exclaimed.

Reuven ignored him. "Take out your new knife," he instructed, "and give me a monk's _tonsure_."

Gavriel stood helplessly while Tarn and Sigurd looked on in amusement.

"Go on," Reuven urged. He produced a cake of mutton fat soap and pointed to a pot of water hanging over the campfire. "Shave my head while the water is hot and enough light remains to see what you're doing!"

For more than an hour Gavriel struggled to denude his uncle's scalp without doing serious damage. He kept cutting the circle unevenly and was forced to broaden it until Reuven was left with only a thin fringe of hair surrounding a ridiculously large bald spot. Tarn and Sigurd laughed and pointed and chattered away as they dipped bread into simmering pottage. Damek sat off to one side, gnawing on salt pork, confused by his master's antics.

Devouring his own supper later, Gavriel peered across the flames at the oddity that was his uncle. Reuven looked far too comfortable in his blasphemous disguise. Gavriel wondered which was more despicable in God's eyes – Reuven eating pork, Reuven wearing a monk's habit, or the crucifix dangling around his own neck. He started to tuck it underneath his tunic but stopped, afraid to let it touch his skin.

Reuven saw him fiddling with the thing and chuckled. "Nephew, what are you worried about? Come, let me tell you a story," he said, downing the last soggy bite of his bread.

CHAPTER EIGHT

Chapter VIII

Imagine a tribe of Jews, riding horseback over vast plains, each man a mighty warrior!"
Suddenly Reuven jumped up. He began to gallop
around the fire, cracking an imaginary whip. "How
on earth did Jews become fierce and expert horsemen of the plains, you ask?"

The startled Swedes stared open-mouthed at
the crazy Jew in the monk's habit.

"But the better question is, 'How did a nomadic
tribe of fierce and expert horsemen become Jews?'"
Reuven stopped, out of breath, resting hands on
knees to recover.

Sigurd elbowed Tarn and they both chortled.

But Reuven wasn't finished. "Let me tell you,
Nephew, about these bold and fierce Khazars. They
wandered back and forth over the plains beside the
Black Sea, a proud and independent people – heathens, all!"

Gavriel, who knew the story well, felt hot
beneath the dumbfounded stares of Damek and the
Northmen. "Shh! Uncle Reuven, please sit down. I've

heard it before."

His embarrassed plea went unheeded. Reuven rose dramatically, an elongated figure in the firelight, arms outstretched. "The Khazars had a king – the fastest rider of them all – skilled with bow and arrow, dressed in felt boots with bronze buckles. He wore baggy trousers, golden earrings and long braids. A day came when he wanted to choose a religion for his people, but in his heathen ignorance he had no idea which faith was the true one. So he called before him a Jew, a Muslim, and a Christian."

Mystified and a little unsettled by the steady stream of Hebrew and the speaker's theatrics, Tarn rose and backed into the shadows. He rested a cautious hand on the hilt of his sword.

"Reuven! I told you, I *know* this story," hissed Gavriel. "Please, come and sit down."

But Reuven was lost in the wonder of the legend. He began to strut like a proud warrior king. "'Each of you must explain your religion to me,' the Khazar king commanded the three. And so they did. But the wise king then decided to question them separately. He called the Christian before him and said, 'If you had to choose between being a Muslim and being a Jew, which would you choose?'"

Now Reuven switched to the role of the Christian, a part for which he was already perfectly dressed. He raised the hood of his habit. "Sire, I could never be a Muslim, for it is a false religion, and odious. I would choose the Jewish faith."

Next Reuven dropped to his knees and mimicked a Muslim touching his forehead to the ground in prayer. Tarn returned to the circle of light and slapped Sigurd on the back. He pointed at Reuven and the two roared with laughter, exposing missing teeth. Damek sat still as a stone, his eyes following Reuven's every move.

To Gavriel's dismay, the play continued. "The Muslim said, 'Sire, the Christian faith is odious to me, for though Christians say they believe in one God, they really believe in three, whom they call the Father, Son and Holy Spirit! I would never even consider being a Christian, therefore if I had to choose, I would choose the Jewish faith.'"

Gavriel sighed. Obviously Reuven intended to perform the story to its end. Well, what did it matter if a couple of uncouth Northmen made sport of his uncle? They were clearly enjoying themselves now, pointing and chattering as if trying to guess what the Jew would do next.

Reuven leapt to his feet. "Then the Khazar king called the Jew before him and posed the same question. The Jew wrestled in thought until he was exhausted. At last he declared, 'Sire, I would choose neither Islam nor Christianity. The Jewish faith is the only true faith and to embrace another is unthinkable to me. Therefore I *will not* choose.' And so, at that moment the Khazar king knew that he had found the true faith – a faith that bends its knee to no other." Reuven gave a dramatic bow and waved both hands with a flourish.

A moment of stunned silence followed. Two bats darted through the clearing; the only sound was the gentle lapping of the Saône against its banks. Finally

Sigurd raised a fist and cheered raucously. Tarn joined in. Even Damek, his face awash with relief, cracked a smile.

Reuven took a second bow. Sigurd handed him his sword and stalked off to wrap himself in a wool blanket and sleep on a bed of fir needles. Tarn lingered a while, dubious about leaving the crazy Jew to guard the camp during the night's first watch. But fatigue finally persuaded him, and he, too, bedded down.

"Gavriel," said Reuven, "even though I feel compelled to disguise myself now and then in the interests of safety, rest assured that I am like the Jew in the story. I will never embrace Islam or Christianity. I am a Jew, through and through. One God, one religion."

Gavriel eyed his uncle's shadowy form and the handsome face glowing faint in the dying fire's light. "Nevertheless," he mumbled, "I'm glad Rabbi Maimon cannot see me wearing this ... this ... *thing* around my neck."

⁕ ⁕ ⁕

"We're nearing the Rhine River," remarked Reuven one day soon after. He sniffed appreciatively at the piney air. "The alps now lie to the south of us and the foggy hills ahead are the beginning of two smaller ranges that run to the north. The Rhine cuts between them. Soon we'll follow a tributary to the great river itself."

The ground flattened out and the forest thinned. The narrow road junctioned with a crumbling stone highway built ages before by the Romans. It led the traders past fields of ripening spelt, barley and feathery, blue-green rye. Rabbits darted through cabbage patches, frightened by the clopping mules and human voices. A skinny, fair-haired boy goading an ox toward a stream paused to watch the travelers as they passed. After casting suspicious glances at the unkempt Northmen, he seemed relieved to see a monk bring up the rear of the procession. Soon Gavriel caught a glimpse of a wide ribbon of silver slicing the landscape in two. It shimmered on the horizon like a snake caught sunning itself.

"There it is!" said Reuven. "The Rhine."

Gavriel's breath caught in his throat. This sparkling smudge on the horizon was so much more than a river to him. It was his gateway to the world, opening onto mystery after mystery. He had dreamed of this moment every day since leaving Cordoba. His feet were sore and calloused; he'd grown leaner and more sinewy on the sparse traveler's diet. His boots were caked with mud. His coarse, itchy garment had grown stiff with dust and dried sweat, but he had done it! Or nearly had.

A beefy man with leathery skin surprised them in the road. Appearing out of nowhere, he wore a black tunic and carried a long-handled axe. "Toll," he said in Frankish, pointing upward to a castle barely visible through a low-hanging cloud. When Reuven balked, he lifted his axe meaningfully, glancing toward another bulky fellow in chainmail, who had just stepped out from behind a thick-trunked spruce.

"How much?" asked Reuven.

"One sou."

"Twelve whole deniers? That's robbery!"

The man with the axe smiled slyly. He eyed the mules and baggage. "We can do robbery, if you prefer."

Irritated, Reuven counted out the silver coins. The man took the money without further comment and let them pass. By the time Gavriel snatched a backward glance, both men had withdrawn into the trees.

They found shelter that afternoon in the hostelry of a stone abbey. Reuven and Gavriel politely declined the simple supper offered by the monks. They left Damek there to eat with the Northmen and wandered into the village of Ottmarsheim, near the banks of the Rhine. Reuven generously offered a fisherman's wife three silver deniers to fry him two trout with fresh herbs. While the shocked woman scurried to comply, Gavriel bought a pricy loaf of wheat bread, hot mulled wine and an onion to add to the woman's iron skillet.

"It's the Sabbath eve, after all," said Reuven. "None of the monks' barley bread and turnip stew for us; we are going to eat in style!"

They carried the food to a cliff overlooking the river. Covering their heads with prayer shawls, they bowed together before eating.

Blessed art thou, oh Lord our God, King of the Universe, who brings forth bread from the earth. They broke the Sabbath loaf and began to consume the sumptuous meal. As they ate they watched the sun slide down the soft blue sky. "No traveling tomorrow," Reuven decided. "We'll spend the Sabbath here, and even Sunday. A rest will do us good."

Gavriel felt comforted and relieved. It was the first time Reuven had observed the Sabbath since the journey's beginning. Only once had he remem-

bered to recite the morning blessings, and only
sporadically did he chant the _Shema Yisrael_ or the
afternoon Psalms. Gavriel had grown accustomed to
saying his daily prayers alone. If Solomon had known
about his brother's spiritual laxity, would he still have
consented to Gavriel's going along? Perhaps Solomon
did know, but had chosen to turn a blind eye for the
sake of allowing his son to fulfill his dreams.... This
thought filled the boy with sudden warmth toward
his faraway father. For the first time he felt a pang
of sympathy for the pain his departure must have
caused. And yet he was filled with gratitude that his
father had let him go.

Below, the Rhine rushed powerfully along, fed
by melting mountain snows and summer rains. A
flock of wild ducks bobbed in the shallows. A leggy
stork strutted across a sandbar. When the sun disappeared, leaving a purplish haze, the Jews retraced
their steps to the abbey. In a corner of the large
hostelry, Sigurd and Damek were already snoring.
Tarn, keeping watch against the possible treachery
of other travelers, gave his usual grunt that meant,
"Good night, sleep well." As Gavriel lay down to
sleep, a heaviness settled in his chest. The reliable
Northman was keeping watch for the last time.

In the morning, Tarn and Sigurd sold their mules
and loaded their baggage onto a northbound boat. As
a parting gift, Tarn emptied a small pouch of amber
pieces into Reuven's hands. Reuven sifted through
the stones, holding one up to the sunlight. Though
unpolished, it glowed with cloudy warmth.

In turn, Reuven presented them with four ells

of purple silk, enough for two women's gowns. The fabric looked oddly out of place in the Northmen's weathered hands as they passed it admiringly between them. They skidded chapped fingers over the sleek cloth and held it appreciatively to their sun burnt faces. What their women looked like, Gavriel could only guess. Were they tall and slender like their men, or short and stocky like Mira and the Slavonic women who served in Baruch's household?

With a final good-bye, Tarn and Sigurd boarded the boat. Its pilot loosed the rope from the piling and shoved off with a long stick. The swift current carried them away too quickly, and Gavriel felt an ache in his throat as they disappeared down the Rhine. Reuven put an arm around his nephew. Having left Damek to guard the baggage, the two strolled into the center of town and sat down on the sunny ledge of a well to watch the goings on.

Dung littered Ottmarsheim's streets, its fetid odor hanging heavy in the air. The houses were squat and roofed with thatch, some of it rotting and worm-infested. A blacksmith's hammer rang out unapologetically on this Sabbath day. Under Gavriel's curious gaze the town's inhabitants went, undistracted, about their chores and errands, obviously used to the sight of travelers.

The Frankish women appeared strong and capable. They walked about in dull-colored linen shifts and head coifs, hauling heavy baskets or *jute* sacks. One red-faced girl wrestled a young pig down the street, tightly gripping its squealing, wriggling flesh, and cursing the unwieldy beast. Gavriel stared after her in amazement. How elegant and pampered were his mother and sisters, with their servants and glittering bracelets and silk gowns! They knew no other life than that of plenty, no other world but bountiful, sunny Sefarad. *And neither did I, until now,* he thought.

At the far end of the muddy main street, a horse appeared, then two. A third joined them. More Knights of the Cross, passing through. A shiver ran down Gavriel's spine. Though clothed as a Christian, he nevertheless felt naked, exposed as a Jew to all who cared to look closely. The knights were far off and going about their own business, but Gavriel could not help feeling unnerved by their presence in town.

"When we've sold the goods," he told his uncle, "I'm going to buy a sword with my cut of the money. A heavy, steel one like Tarn's and Sigurd's."

"A worthwhile purchase, perhaps," Reuven replied. His eyes were closed, his face upturned, absorbing the sun. "I rely on my wits to survive. But a sword could come in handy."

Gavriel, too, closed his eyes, wondering what Solomon would say to his decision to arm himself. *So, now my son would rather kill than heal?*

No! Gavriel answered Solomon's imaginary disapproval. *I want to protect myself, not kill. Try to understand, Father! It's all part of a trader's life.*

꽃 꽃 꽃

Early Monday morning, they engaged a stout

ferryman to transport both man and mule to the
Rhine's opposite shore. It took four trips on his
sturdy raft. Safely across, they regrouped in a village clinging tenuously to the marshy soil and began
the eastward trek. The terrain was wilder over here;
fallen logs blocked the mules' path; their hooves
mired in damp clay. An aged hunter with a pheasant
slung over one shoulder pointed them toward the
overgrown remains of a Roman road. This they followed into thick forest.

Sleep was a luxury they could not afford now
that they traveled alone. After the nightly Frankish
lessons, Reuven and Gavriel took turns dozing while
the other passed the time in tense watchfulness.
By the time four nights and three days had passed,
Gavriel grew edgy. His head ached and his eyes
drooped.

"We're bound to meet up with other travelers going our way," Reuven assured him. "It's high
summer, the time for pilgrimages."

But Gavriel knew most Christian pilgrims
traveled westward and southward, to Santiago de
Compostela, or to southern seaports with ships
bound for the Holy Lands. He and Reuven were
headed in the exact opposite direction.

Nevertheless, Reuven's prediction proved correct. A party of four Benedictine monks overtook
them where the Roman road intersected with a
forest track. 'Greetings, Brother!' they hailed Reuven.

"Now you are caught, Uncle," whispered Gavriel.
With more amusement than fear, he waited for his
uncle's response.

The clever trader met the challenge with ease. In a torrent of Arabic, he stretched his arms wide and embraced his "fellow" Christians. They looked him up and down, muttering to one another. Then Reuven said in broken Latin, "From Spain. Mozarab!"

"Ah!" the face of a freckled monk lit up. He explained something to his companions and they nodded thoughtfully. If they wondered what an Arabic-speaking, Spanish monk was doing with five heavy-laden mules, a Slav and a boy who resembled him enough to be his son, they kept their curiosity under strict control.

Reuven smiled knowingly at Gavriel. It was a great blessing to find trustworthy travel companions, especially along dark forest tracks where bandits lurked. Men of the Church were respected, Reuven assured his nephew, even by outlaws. He patted what appeared to be a paunch but was actually the astrolabe. "Have no doubt; we will reach Ellwangen safely!"

Now the Roman highway climbed gentle hills, dotted with thickets and cultivated fields. The tilled fields gradually turned into grazing lands, then wild meadows scattered between broad swaths of evergreen. The hills rose ever steeper. Here spruce and fir grew so closely together that light hardly penetrated their tangled boughs. This German forest was vast, murky, and menacing. It seemed to Gavriel that he trudged through an endless night.

Bands of travelers passed them going west: a wealthy German widow and her entourage of servants and armed guards, a group of stylishly attired

Frankish traders, German silver miners and a pock-marked lord with four of his knights. A company of lepers, all dressed in black robes and red hats, signaled their approach with wooden castanets. Reuven's party and the monks stepped off the road and watched them pass. The white patches on their robes served to warn others of the men's desperate, incurable disease. No physician could help them. Their hope lay in a constant round of pilgrimages and prayer at Christian shrines. Gavriel turned his eyes away as one of the monks made the sign of the cross over the sad procession.

The Benedictines made pleasant companions. They spoke a guttural Germanic tongue amongst themselves, and Frankish to Reuven. They knew which forest berries and roots were edible. They carried dried yellow peas with them and used them to make thick, hearty stews which they generously shared. Though unarmed, they provided a comforting presence around the campfire, a protective charm against the murky shadows and the howling of wolves.

Squalid villages welcomed the travelers and gladly took their deniers in exchange for food. The inhabitants were hardy, but unwashed and poorly clad, walking about in foul-smelling leather jerkins and trousers. They scratched at scabied skin. Even the young were missing teeth. Each village boasted a simple wooden church and often the local priest came out to greet the monks. These remote Churchmen were especially curious about the Mozarab monk who spoke but few words of Latin.

Most of the time they offered shelter and food, but
if a priest became too inquisitive, Reuven shook his
head as if he didn't understand Latin very well, and
reverted to Arabic.

"Are they all like this?" Gavriel asked his uncle
one day as they bought bread from a market stall.
The corners of the baker's mouth were food encrusted, and his fingernails black with filth. He counted on
his fingers when figuring the weight and price of the
loaf.

Reuven kept smiling at the man as he answered
in Hebrew, "They are only one step above barbar-
ians. Of course, as we both know, your father is full
of gracious theories as to why they live in ignorance."
A puny boy Gavriel took to be the baker's son poked
his nose above the shelf. His hazel eyes observed
every detail of the strangers' faces. Gavriel felt a stab
of pity for the child, grimy and disheveled as he was.
His yellow hair was matted and caked with dust.

"You mean what he said about King Charles?"

Reuven reached into his purse and tossed the
boy a silver denier. Wide-eyed, the child tugged at
his father's jerkin and proudly showed it to him. The
baker flashed the Jew a grateful, gap-toothed smile.

"Well, he was right," Reuven admitted.
"Remember that thug that extorted money from us
on the road? The lord of that castle is getting rich off
travelers like us and the sweat of peasants like these.
These poor, unwashed souls you see are little more
than slaves to the lords that own the land they live
on."

"And *that's* why they're ignorant," whispered

Gavriel, feeling as if the candle his father had tried to light within his mind had finally burst into flame.

"Absolutely," replied Reuven, lowering his voice to match his nephew's whisper. "What good are educated slaves? Would *I* educate Damek, or Aziz?"

Discreetly Gavriel observed the baker's daughter as she punched a lump of dough on a table behind the stall. Her bright eyes shifted constantly from one place to another, taking in everything around her. *Does this illiterate village girl,* he wondered, *ever wish to fill her mind with knowledge? Could someone like her ever really hope to learn to read?* He thought of Shifra and tried to imagine what the two females might say to one another if their paths and languages ever mingled – but he knew they never would.

CHAPTER NINE

Chapter IX

Though July had arrived, the days were often damp, with misty clouds hanging low, drifting just above the treetops. Gavriel longed for sunshine. He tried to push the luxurious warmth of al-Andalus from his memory, focusing instead on the gray and red squirrels darting across his path and up tree trunks. Such delightful creatures he had never known existed! Woodlarks and tree sparrows twittered in the green boughs; hawks and falcons soared over clearings, diving for mice and voles. This ancient forest, so terrifying by night, was bursting with life and by day became a captivating wonderland.

The monks' journey ended at a town called Mengen. Their loss came as a bitter blow, but Reuven was determined to waste no time in pressing on toward Ellwangen. "We will surely meet up with other travelers," he reasoned. "I have traversed these lands before; I'm confident that I know what I'm doing. There's no point in slowing our progress now that we are getting so close to our destination."

And so they continued. The mules were still

strong; food was plentiful. Gavriel, Reuven and Damek had been blessed with good health so far, a sure sign of the Almighty's blessing on their journey and on the sale of the astrolabe.

One night they were startled by a fierce grunting and snorting. Into the fire's glow stepped a hairy swine with curved tusks. The creature froze as if mesmerized, and began to sniff the air. Then he shattered the night with a hideous squeal, turned tail and ran. Away with him thundered the hooves of what sounded like a herd of thirty or more.

Damek leapt up, exclaiming excitedly in Slavonic. Reuven and Gavriel stared at him, uncomprehending. Damek brought his hands to his face, curling his fingers like tusks. He gripped an imaginary spear and made a thrusting motion.

"Yes, yes," Reuven chuckled. "You kill one of those, and we'll eat it!" He joined in the pantomime, pretending to devour meat off a bone.

Damek shook his head and shrugged helplessly.

"This Slav," said Reuven, "is no doubt familiar with the hideous beasts. His native land lies far to the east, but these evergreen forests stretch all the way there. It must put him in a homesick frame of mind."

"I wonder why he doesn't abandon us and flee," mused Gavriel. "I would, if I were him."

"He trusts us," said Reuven. "I promised to free him, and he's counting on it."

"Free him for what? To try to make his way alone in a foreign land? He doesn't even speak Arabic."

Reuven shrugged and said offhandedly, "We must all make our way in life."

꙰ꙮ ꙰ꙮ ꙰ꙮ

They happened one afternoon upon a lonely herdsman's hut, situated at the top of a meadow. After driving stakes into the ground to tether the mules, Reuven, Gavriel and Damek ate a leisurely supper and bedded down in the crude shelter. It felt blessedly safe to lie between four walls instead of out in the open. Gavriel fell asleep and dreamed of feasting – not on the bland pottage and rye breads of these northern lands, but on the spiced, exotic foods he'd once known as everyday fare. In his dream, an olive turned to an ember in his mouth and began to taste of smoke. *Why does Mira fry the olives?* he asked the phantom-like presence of his mother. *See how she has burnt them!* He watched Mira turn the black olives in a pan until the smoke thickened and obscured her from his view. He tasted grit on his tongue and smoke stung his nostrils. With a wheezing, gag-like cough, Gavriel awoke to a wall of fire. One whole side of the herdsman's hut was taken in flame.

"Reuven!" he called. He thrashed out of his tangled blanket and lunged for the door, colliding with Damek.

Reuven stumbled out after them. The earth trembled beneath the heavy clopping of horses' hooves. Dark shapes darted toward the burning hut and burst inside, howling victoriously.

"Fiends!" Reuven croaked between coughs, and at last Gavriel understood that they were being robbed.

Someone hurled the baggage out of the hut, piece by piece. Each pack landed with a heavy thump on the grass. Enraged, coughing and groaning with agony, Reuven beat the ground with one fist. Behind him the hut blazed. Tears stung Gavriel's eyes and nose and a gagging cough nearly strangled him. He groped for his uncle's hand and pulled him farther from the raging flames. Wheezing, their lungs burning, they collapsed in the cool meadow.

A shadowy yet familiar figure abandoned the loot pile and approached them. In the lurid firelight, the knight Garin loomed like an elongated giant. He drew his sword. His face dripped with sweat and he wiped it with a dirty sleeve. He glared down contemptuously at his victims while a chaotic scene played out behind him. Four of the mules had yanked their tether poles clean out of the ground and were roaming free across the meadow. Someone was chasing them down, cursing at the top of his voice.

"Round up every last beast, Robert!" Garin shouted.

In the melée, Gavriel saw Damek struggle to his feet and dart into the forest. Inspired, he clawed at the earth, desperate to find his own feet and flee. Yet he was too dizzy, too disoriented to save himself. The sharp tip of Garin's sword between his shoulder blades stopped him. He collapsed onto his belly. Beside him, Reuven convulsed in a coughing fit.

Gavriel felt his hands jerked behind him, the

wrists strangled with rope. Next, Garin seized Reuven's hands and wound hemp tightly around them. The knight tied uncle and nephew together, back to back, and left them squatting on the ground.

The vanquished hut collapsed and turned to charcoal, glowing brightly with each gust of night wind. Smoke left a gritty film on tongue and skin and a burnt stench deeply embedded in clothing. Throughout the wee hours of the morning, the thieves pawed through the baggage. Grubby hands unrolled _ell_ after ell of silk. Soot-smudged noses sniffed at costly perfumes and spices. Garin and one of his companions bent greedily over the loot, reveling in their conquest. Gavriel began to weep.

"Stop it!" chided Reuven over his shoulder. "Don't let them see your weakness."

Gavriel gnawed his lip and choked back the tears. In all Reuven's vast experience on the road, had he ever encountered anything like this? His uncle spoke with defiant bravado, but Gavriel could feel him trembling.

༈ ༈ ༈

The sun rose on a disastrous mess. The hut lay in a charred, smoking heap. The meadow was strewn with trampled jute sacks and ransacked leather satchels. Vials of medicinal powders and perfume dotted the grass, some of them broken, spilling expensive scent onto the ground, its sickening sweetness mingling with the lingering smoke. The horses and mules grazed peacefully. Garin's companions lay snoring, wrapped in Reuven's silk. Bernard was surrounded by empty wine flasks. Garin sat against a fir trunk at the forest's edge, ogling the rare prize in his hands – the jeweled astrolabe from Fez. During the night, Garin had made a thorough search of his captives. In so doing, the knight had not only stripped Reuven of his money purse but stumbled upon the most magnificent treasure he had ever laid eyes on. When Garin slit the pouch and removed the astrolabe, Reuven had been unable to heed his own advice, and wept aloud.

The knight had entirely ignored the crucifix around Gavriel's neck. It made sense. Why should the grasping Garin care about a bit of carved olivewood? Hands firmly bound, Gavriel thought with bitter irony, *My disguise is useless now, and yet I am forced to continue wearing this idolatrous trinket! Perhaps this, too, is a punishment for impersonating a Christian. I should never have let Reuven talk me into it!*

Gavriel watched Garin rise heavily on mud-splattered boots and tramp across the meadow. He kicked his two companions awake. "Bernard! Harness the mules. Robert, repack the goods and load the baggage onto the beasts."

Slight, skittish Robert jumped to obey Garin's command. Bernard kicked off his silk blanket and sat in a dazed stupor. By the looks of things, the man had drained several wine flasks during the night. He groaned, holding his head in both hands.

Garin approached the prisoners and taunted in clumsy Arabic, "Did you really think to fool people with that monk's habit? Anyone can see you are Jews."

Reuven replied with exhausted calm, "And anyone can see that you are a Christian."

Unsure whether this was an insult or just a reference to the faded cross on his tunic, Garin screwed up his face for a moment. Finally he shook his head as if to clear away the confusion.

Reuven looked boldly into his captor's eyes. "Did the abbot dismiss you from his entourage, or did you desert him?"

"What, Peter of Cluny?" Garin smirked. "I feel no loyalty toward him. That Muslim lover doesn't even support the _Crusades_!"

Bernard approached, wiping gritty hands on his tunic. He was solid of build and had a tanned complexion, made even darker by soot. "And what about these?"

Garin replied gloatingly, "It's a well known fact that Jews pay ransom for their captive Jew brothers."

"And where will we find those Jews?"

Garin pursed his lips and gazed skyward, thinking hard. "I suppose at ... Augsburg. There were plenty of them there last time I passed through."

"What! To Augsburg, then? You said we were going west, to Paris!"

"Well now we're headed to Augsburg. I'm not waiting until Paris to get a ransom for these dogs."

Bernard belched and again gripped his head with both hands. On his finger sparkled Reuven's ruby ring. He turned away, muttering a curse, and stalked off toward the mules.

Trussed up like chickens awaiting slaughter, Reuven and Gavriel shuffled along behind the last mule. Garin had found Reuven's black caftan among the baggage and made him wear it, saying, "The locals would surely object to a captive monk, but to captive Jews, never!"

They walked for three days, thankful for the plodding pace of the mules. The hemp chafed at their wrists. The road to Augsburg was well traveled, but those who passed or overtook them stared at Reuven and Gavriel with loathing, as if certain they were criminals.

"Will no one pity a captive Jew?" muttered Gavriel as he trudged along.

"Obviously not," Reuven panted. "Can't you see we're like dogs to them? The Christians hate us."

Occasionally, the prisoners were allowed to relieve themselves in the forest while kept on a tether, then quickly yanked back in line behind the procession. At evening campfire they were made to lap up their pottage like beasts, for Garin refused to untie their hands. Throughout each long evening they were forced to watch Garin and Bernard paw greedily through their possessions, exclaiming over the astrolabe and planning how to spend the deniers its sale would bring them. During such times Robert often took pity on the hapless Jews, holding a cup of cool water to their lips. But then, at Garin's bidding, he would bind their feet tightly so that they could not escape during the night.

Gavriel lost track of the days. Damp mornings and dusty afternoons blended together in a never-ending cycle of aching legs, hunger and exhaustion. His skin itched maddeningly. Even when Robert poured water between his chapped lips, he could never swallow enough to satisfy his raging thirst. He felt hope slipping away, but tried to keep it alive by dwelling on his destination. "Will the Jews of Augsburg really ransom us?" he asked Reuven in Hebrew. "We are complete strangers to them."

"*If* there are any Jews left in Augsburg at all, I have no doubt they will pay a ransom."

Gavriel glared sideways at his uncle, whose normally smooth-shaven face was now covered with beard stubble. "What do you mean, *if* there are any Jews left?"

"Didn't you know? Jews are being driven out of the Rhinelands and pushed eastward by Crusader ruffians like our 'friends' here." He cut his eyes bitterly toward his captors, who rode on horseback at the head of the procession. "It's been going on for years now. Few Jews remain in these parts."

Burning rage scorched Gavriel's cheeks and forehead. An image flashed through his mind of pummeling his uncle's arrogant face with hard fists. The violent thought shocked him. Yet try as he might, he could not quell the force surging within him. "You never said a word about that! Why did you bring me here, when you knew we could never get out alive?"

"Because I've managed to travel the Rhinelands before and you can see perfectly well that I survived!"

"You think you know everything, don't you? You always have a trick, a scheme, an answer up your sleeve, but look at you now!"

"Yes, look at me! I've lost *everything*. Losing that astrolabe has been the greatest financial disaster of my life! Do you know how many dirhams I invested in it?"

Gavriel ground his teeth in impotent fury. "All you care about is money."

The two lapsed into tense silence. They marched on, listening to the rattle of woodpeckers and the mules' clopping. After a while, Reuven quietly conceded, "The things you say are true. I must find a way to make it right. And we must *both* beg the Holy One for mercy."

Gavriel almost retorted that a Jew who posed as a Muslim and a Christian, who devoured pork and who often disregarded the Sabbath had no business begging for mercy. Yet he knew all too well that this contentious bickering with Reuven would not help the situation. With effort he drove the resentment from his voice and queried, "Should we try to escape?"

Reuven laughed bitterly. "Two penniless, unarmed Jews wandering around a German forest? It would be only a matter of time before someone else preyed upon us. No, we are safer with these brutes, provided there are Jews in Augsburg to redeem us."

CHAPTER TEN

Chapter X

hat night Garin caught Reuven's chin
with the tip of his sword and lifted his face. "I have
killed my share of Christ-killers," he arrogantly
confessed. "The Pope promised me forgiveness of
all my sins if I would take up the sword for the holy
cause and fight the infidels. I was a Templar; now I'm
a *mercenary*, working for whoever offers me the most
pay. During ten years in the Holy Land I killed both
Muslim and Jew. Neither is worthy to live in the land
of Christ, and walk where he walked."

"Rest assured," Reuven retorted, "we have no
intention of walking *there*. We ask only to walk freely
here."

"Shut up! You're lucky to still walk at all.
When you say your Jew prayers, ask God to make
your brothers in Augsburg willing to ransom you.
Otherwise you have reached your end."

Reuven and Gavriel huddled close together and
began to recite the familiar Shema. *Hear oh Israel!
The Lord is our God, the Lord is One. You shall love
Adonai your God with all your heart, with all your soul,*

and with all your might. And these words which I com-
mand you today shall be in your heart. You shall teach
them diligently to your children and you shall speak of
them when you are sitting at home and when you go on
a journey, when you lie down and when you rise up ...
and they shall be jewels between your eyes....

When they had finished, Reuven wiped moist
eyes with his sleeve and whispered, "Nephew, if you
do not make it back home alive, how will I ever face
Solomon? I have always looked up to him; never in
my life would I have done anything to hurt him! But
now I have stolen his only son away, and for what?
For disaster and daily threat of death at the hands of
these ... these ... "

"I was a disappointment to my father," Gavriel
whispered back. "You didn't cause *that.*"

With a tear-choked sob, Reuven replied,
"Perhaps not, but I made things worse. I, of all people!
How well I know what it's like to be a disappointment; my physician father gave me my freedom even
as my brother gave you yours. But he would much
rather have seen me follow in his footsteps. Oh, mine
has been an empty life," he moaned. "I didn't realize
until now just how empty it truly was, chasing after
money rather than a life of healing like my brother's."

The knights took brief notice of the weeping
Reuven, and with profound indifference returned to
their supper.

Trembling, Gavriel placed a tentative hand on
his uncle's shoulder. It shook him deeply to see this
confident man in the grip of despair. He tried to
speak, but faltered. He had never seen this side of

Reuven, never imagined it existed. *How can I possibly comfort him,* he thought, *when I am terrified myself?* "What's done is done," he whispered, keeping a watchful eye on Garin. "And your life hasn't been so bad! You said yourself that without traders, a physician in al-Andalus would have no camphor, no opium...."

But Reuven was beyond human comfort. "Oh Holy One, forgive me," he wailed. "From now on, I promise to live a better life. I promise to devote myself to a career that will bring honor to my father, may he rest!"

To Gavriel's relief, Reuven finally dropped his head on his knees and whimpered quietly to himself.

Robert brought the dregs of the knights' supper, setting the pot down between the two captives. For the first time he untied the Jews' hands, and guarded them carefully as they scooped the cooled stew to their mouths. This act of mercy, paltry as it was, brought sharp, stinging tears to Gavriel's eyes.

Throughout the long twilight, uncle and nephew each remained lost in his own thoughts. Gradually, the treetops faded into the darkening sky. Soon the softly bending branches disappeared into blackness. The Jews' captors began to yawn. Bernard banked the fire and all three knights stumbled off to sleep.

But sleep would not come to Gavriel. Lying beside Reuven on the hard ground, he whispered, "Tell me Uncle, if we Jews are the children of God – his chosen people – then why are we hounded by Mohammedan fanatics on one side and Christian

fanatics on the other? Do Jews persecute either of
them? No! Why doesn't the way things *are* reflect
what we believe – that the Jews are the apple of
God's eye?"

Reuven was quiet for so long that Gavriel
thought he had fallen asleep. When at last he spoke,
he startled the boy. "Have faith, Gavriel. A person
with faith believes what he cannot see with his own
eyes. Take Abraham, for instance – God promised to
make his descendants into a great nation. He didn't
see that happen, but he believed. So *we* believe."

Gavriel thrashed from side to side, unable to
find a comfortable position. If only he could speak to
Rabbi Maimon! Contrite though he was this evening, the flamboyant, worldly Reuven was still the
last person Gavriel thought of as a spiritual guide.
Yet there was no one else to talk to ... no one else
to whom he could pose the question that refused to
stop haunting him. "How can I have faith, Uncle? I
see Jews under attack at every turn, and so I must
conclude that the Holy One is *not* on our side. But
you still believe that we Jews are his chosen people!"

Reuven sighed. "Learned scholars from the
Levant to al-Andalus ponder this question every day
and never seem to arrive at a satisfactory answer.
And you expect *me* to clarify it for you? Go to sleep!"

Reuven, rolled onto his back and soon began
to snore, leaving Gavriel to wrestle with his doubts.
When the wrestling had exhausted him, he too fell
asleep.

A loud crack awoke him. His eyes strained at
the darkness but he could see nothing. The sun

merely hinted at rising, spreading a swath of pale light through spruce boughs. There came another crack of twigs under a heavy step, then a grunt and a scuffle. Sharp curses echoed off the trees.

"Uncle Reuven!" Gavriel groped for his uncle's shoulder and shook him hard.

Someone crashed across the clearing, banging into the cooking pot suspended over a dead fire. A shadowy figure charged after him. Swords clashed.

"You thieving wretch! Give it back!" snarled Garin.

"I don't take orders from you anymore!"

"Who says you don't? You *will* obey me!"

Bernard and Garin careened closer to the Jews as they exchanged furious blows in the darkness. Gavriel rolled backward, slamming against a fir trunk. Reuven struggled to his knees and shuffled forward, trying to wedge himself between Gavriel and danger. A whirring steel blade sliced the air just above their heads.

An ear-shattering scream filled the forest.

Someone fell with a heavy thud. Footsteps pounded across the clearing. A horse whinnied, then thundered off into the trees. The world hushed until an agonized groan rose out of the shadows.

"Garin?" It was Robert's timid voice. "Are you wounded?"

In reply there came a hoarse, "He cut me!"

"I'll help you! Don't move ... lie still...." Panicked, the young knight stumbled toward Garin's voice, tripping over the fire pit and setting a few banked embers aglow. "Light!" he cried. "We need light!"

He crouched over the dormant fire and attempted to blow it to life. A few embers sputtered and took flame. Robert scooped fir needles and cones onto the fire and fanned it desperately. Soon it grew strong enough to receive a piece of hewn log.

In the weak light, the Jews watched Robert kneel beside a mountain of flesh. Garin lay on his side, curled up tight and moaning in agony. He was covered with blood.

"Lord Jesus and Saint Peter, receive his soul. Receive his soul, Lord Jesus," jabbered Robert, utterly beside himself.

This is it! thought Gavriel. Reuven tensed and he knew his uncle was thinking the same thing. If Garin died of his wounds, they could overpower the frightened, grieving Robert. Gavriel began to work his wrists, trying desperately to loosen the hemp.

But Reuven had something else in mind.

"This boy is a physician!" he shouted above Robert's hysterical prayers. "Let him take a look at the knight's wounds."

Gavriel felt the breath strangle in his throat. Had Reuven gone completely mad?

Another pitiful groan from the wounded man brought Robert to his feet. In desperation he approached the captives, throwing uncertain glances between them and the bleeding Garin.

"I speak the truth," Reuven assured him. "My nephew studied under the finest doctors in Cordoba."

Robert hesitated. Gavriel felt sick, as though his uncle had kicked him in the kidneys. Garin groaned, "Oh God, receive my soul...."

Robert drew his knife and cut loose Gavriel's bonds. His wrists raw from the chafing hemp, Gavriel stumbled forward. He stopped. Had Reuven meant the offer of help as a ruse? Should he run at Robert, take him by surprise? Another glance at Reuven convinced him his uncle meant for him to do exactly what he had promised. So this was how Reuven meant to make right his wrongs! Or had the fear of imminent death truly revived his uncle's piety? Whatever the reason, Reuven's face had mitzvah written all over it. *Why can't you perform your own good deeds?* thought Gavriel acidly, but the unexpected sincerity on Reuven's face caught him off guard and made him ashamed. With a fluttering in his belly, he approached the patient.

The sun was beginning to turn the sky red, but Gavriel needed more light. He motioned for Robert to feed the fire. The knight hastened to obey. From a few steps off, Gavriel could see that Bernard's sword had slit Garin's tunic and lacerated his abdomen. His left hand was missing the two smallest fingers, leaving bloody stumps. The boy's stomach reeled at the sight of gaping, yellowish fat and coursing blood. He shut his eyes and forced air into his lungs in a steady rhythm. What was it Nizar al-Jady had said beside the maristan fountain that day?

Your mind must master your stomach.

Gavriel envisioned the cool, bubbling water, tried to imagine it dripping onto his dust-streaked face, cooling his feverish brain, calming his roiling stomach. He lurched forward as if Nizar himself had pushed him toward the bloodied patient.

"I will need his help," said Gavriel, pointing at Reuven. But he had spoken in Arabic, and Robert only gaped at him, uncomprehending.

Reuven repeated the words in Frankish. Alarmed, Robert drew his knife and took a backward step.

"I am also the son of a physican," Reuven reassured him. "I am able to help."

At last accepting that he had no choice, Robert untied Reuven. The skinny knight dropped his knife and sank onto the ground beside it, as if expecting at any moment to be attacked and overpowered.

But Gavriel and Reuven had no time for him. Gavriel knelt by Garin's side. He took a deep breath and braced himself. "Tie a tourniquet around his arm," he instructed Reuven. "And find me a needle and a flask of wine."

Nothing came easily. The thieves had shoved medical supplies, spices, silks and perfumes willy-nilly back into the baggage. Reuven clawed his way through the jumbled goods until he found a clean length of silk. He bit and tore until he had a scrap suitable for a tourniquet. While Gavriel explored the abdominal wound left by Bernard's treachery, Reuven delved further into the baggage. Fortunately, a small pouch of needles remained undisturbed at the bottom of what had once been Gavriel's new travel satchel.

Gavriel used one of Garin's own leather gloves to snatch a glowing lump of charcoal from the fire. Squeezing his eyes shut, he held the hand firmly and pressed it onto the bleeding finger stumps to cauterize them. His gut wrenched at the sizzle of human flesh. Garin went rigid and screamed in agony.

"Pack warm ashes onto the hand," he told his uncle. "Hold them down tight and wrap the hand in cloth."

Human hair was needed for the most arduous task. Robert's was straight and hung to his shoulders. But when Gavriel plucked a few strands from the surprised knight's head, he sighed in disappointment. The blondish hairs were brittle and useless. Instinctively, he laid a hand on the man's neck. "I knew it," he murmured as he felt the telltale lump. Robert tensed with fear, but Gavriel was too lost in a memory to reassure him.

"*Can you feel it?*" asked al-Jady, guiding Gavriel's hand along the neck of a patient in the maristan. "*If the lump continues to grow, the patient's hair will become brittle. Eventually his eyes will bulge; he will not be able to stand the heat of a normal day.*" "*And what is the treatment?*" Nizar queried. Al-Jady shook his head sadly. "*For this, we have no treatment.*"

Somehow the echo of familiar voices gave him strength to face what lay in front of him. Gavriel returned to the patient on the ground and swabbed the edges of the wound with wine. He plucked one of his own coarse, wavy hairs and threaded it into the needle. Bernard's sword had sliced deep. In one spot a shiny section of bowel was visible, but to Gavriel's relief, the blade had missed the vital organ. Only muscle and flesh needed to be sewn together. Gavriel shivered, flushed hot, then felt icy pinpricks on the skin of his face as he inserted the needle and began to stitch.

Robert and Reuven struggled to hold the patient still. Their task became easier as the wounded man weakened from blood loss. Garin clenched his teeth and moaned. Soon he lost consciousness and lay limp in their arms.

Gavriel's fingers fumbled at first. But as he

sewed on, his clumsy hands grew steadier and
stopped shaking. The wound stretched from the left
hip to the navel. It seemed to Gavriel he would never
reach the end, because he had to stop constantly
and re-thread the needle. But he worked steadily on,
making small, neat stitches, stopping often to take
deep breaths and summon the image of the cool,
bubbling fountain and Nizar's urgent voice.

When at last the wound was securely closed, he
handed the bloody needle to Reuven. "Swab the abdomen again with wine," he said, and stumbled into
the forest to vomit.

꙰ꙮ   ꙰ꙮ   ꙰ꙮ

They remained at the makeshift camp for three
days. During that time, Robert kept faithful watch by
Garin's side. One sunny afternoon, Gavriel sat down
beside the young knight, watching the patient sleep.
Hearing Robert whisper a prayer, Gavriel suddenly
remembered the wooden crucifix still dangling from
his neck. Inspiration struck him. He slipped the pendant over his head and dropped it into Robert's lap.

Startled, Robert looked up at the Jew.

"You can keep it," said Gavriel, in his stumbling,
awkward Frankish. He also made use of hand signals
to add, "You can hold onto it while you pray."

The unexpected gesture unleashed something
in Robert. Tears welled up in his eyes and spilled
over his cheeks as he clutched the cross tightly. "I
never hated Jews," he sobbed. "I never even hated
Mohammedans. I only knew that the Holy Lands had

been overrun by Muslims, and my Christian brothers and sisters there were desperate to be freed. I wanted to help make the way safe again for Christian pilgrims going to Jerusalem. I swear I only wanted to honor my Lord Jesus Christ and fight bravely for his sake! But when I got there, I saw so much cruelty and bloodshed. How could such a just cause go so awry?"

Taken aback by the torrent of words, Gavriel looked helplessly at Reuven. His uncle wasted no time in translating Robert's words into Arabic. Gavriel felt a flood of pity for the penitent knight. He, of all people, knew about Muslim oppression. Wouldn't he have liked to wrest Cordoba out of Almoravid hands, making it safe for his fellow Jews, even as this young Frank longed to free the Holy Lands? Not knowing what to say, he patted the weeping fellow on the shoulder in mute sympathy.

By the third day, Garin's sutured wound began to clot and knit together. Reuven and Robert fashioned a hammock out of many layers of silk and slung it between two mules. In this way Garin rode to Ulm. The whole way he cursed Bernard and begged repeatedly for the tortuous journey to halt. His misery finally ended at a Benedictine monastery, where monks received him into their hostelry. It was a strange, bedraggled party of men that delivered him there – a swarthy Jew with ragged tonsure, a mule train packing the soiled and tattered remnants of a trader's cargo, a subdued young knight and a youthful physician who gave orders to the astonished monks.

They laid Garin on a pallet in a corner of the

hospice room, where the only other patient was an elderly woman who slept deeply, emitting echoing snores. Gavriel lifted Garin's tunic to reveal the sutured cut. The monks gasped. "Cleanse it three times daily with strong wine," he told them, "and pack it in camphor. If it should become infected, apply the juice of a raw onion."

The monks gabbled amongst themselves in a mixture of Germanic and Latin as they inspected the finger stumps. Seeing them ash-blackened but healing well, the brothers looked upon the young Jew with sincere admiration. Garin himself expressed no gratitude toward his Jewish saviors. Relief washed over his pale, puffy face as he took in his surroundings, and he moaned pitifully, "Help me, brothers! My astrolabe has been stolen!"

Robert accompanied the Jews to the center of Ulm, where they arranged to join other travelers on the road to Augsburg. "How can I possibly thank you," said the young knight, clasping Gavriel's hand. "You see, Garin is my half brother, and I promised our father I would stick by him. He would surely have died if you had not been with us."

Looking squarely into Robert's grateful eyes, Gavriel understood for the first time in his life what mitzvah truly was. It felt good to understand and it felt good to be a Jew. He clasped the young knight's hand in farewell.

"Ah, mitzvah!" exclaimed Reuven, unknowingly giving voice to his nephew's thoughts. He threw up both hands as if to say the mystery was too great for anyone to comprehend.

Robert smiled at the strange Hebrew word. "I know you are Jews," he said. "But I pray Christ's blessings upon you both."

As Gavriel gave Robert's hand a final farewell squeeze, his eyes fell on the swollen neck. He wished mightily that he could heal Robert from a disease he didn't even know he had. But not even hakims like Solomon or al-Jady knew what to do for such an ailment, for they did not know what caused it. *Perhaps one day I will know,* he thought.

The road to Augsburg from Ulm was short and safely traveled, for the Jews joined up with a large company of travelers.

"How ironic!" commented Reuven bitterly. "Now that we have nothing worth stealing, we are well protected!"

Augsburg's handful of Jews received the weary travelers with warm hospitality. They offered mats and blankets and a quiet corner of the synagogue in which to sleep. These Jews spoke a Germanic jargon amongst themselves, but their knowledge of Hebrew bridged the gap between them and their Andalusian brothers. They had some strange customs. Their women haggled boldly in the marketplace and did not veil their faces. Yet Jews were Jews, and it comforted Gavriel to rest at long last among his own people.

Reuven sold the mules and the tattered remnants of his cargo, but the goods were so damaged they brought only weak prices. The Augsburg Jews, though living from day to day in a state of uncertainty, took up a collection to help their destitute brothers return home.

⚜ ⚜ ⚜

For their journey, Reuven and Gavriel dressed neither as Jews nor Churchmen, but wore the plain garb of Spanish peasants. They spoke Andalusi and kept to themselves. No one bothered them. When in the chill of November they crossed the Pyrenees into Spanish territory and heard Arabic spoken by both Muslim, Jew and Mozarab Christian, they fell and kissed the ground.

Once in Toledo, Reuven sought out the *nagid* of the Jewish community, hoping to question him about a Jew's prospects in the city. As he spilled the entire story of disaster and loss, the elderly man lent him a sympathetic ear. "I just need to get on my feet again," Reuven informed the Jewish leader. "But once I do, I have a plan to import camphor from China; maybe a little amber from the north."

Gavriel's mouth dropped open.

Avoiding Gavriel's incredulous stare, Reuven said quickly, "Most honored Nagid, allow me to introduce my nephew, Gavriel ben Solomon Zafrani of Cordoba."

The old fellow's eyes widened. "Gavriel *ben Solomon Zafrani?*" he repeated, combing gnarled fingers through a gray-streaked beard. "Do you mean to say you are the son of Solomon ben Judah Zafrani, the physician who has just moved here from Cordoba?"

Reuven and Gavriel exchanged shocked looks.

"My father? In Toledo?"

"So he took my advice after all!" Reuven exulted.

Finding his family in Toledo was more than Gavriel could have hoped for. He thought he would drown in a flood of joy! The Zafranis were already thriving, living in an imposing stone house in the Jewish quarter. All the household servants had come along. When Gavriel entered the front door for the first time, Rohel smothered her son in a crushing embrace and Solomon wept openly.

"Ruined! I am utterly ruined!" wailed Reuven, launching into a mournful recitation of the calamitous journey. "How will I ever be able to buy the house I dreamed of? Devorah and I and the children will be reduced to beggary! Every dirham I invested in the astrolabe is lost. This disaster has almost finished me as a trader! And to think I traded a faithful Muslim slave for a Christian Slav who deserted me in my hour of need! But I have a plan; don't you worry! It will surely take some time to recover my loss, but I have a plan."

At Reuven's tale of woe, Rohel hugged Gavriel tighter, exclaiming, "And through all *that*, the Holy One preserved the life of my only son!"

Gavriel basked in the fond attentions of his mother and sisters. They brought him stuffed hen on a platter, wild asparagus and cakes made from dates and almonds. When he had eaten his fill and taken a long overdue bath, he reclined drowsily on a row of soft cushions.

Solomon came and sat beside him. "How grateful I am that you passed through Toledo and found us here," he said. "We asked Rabbi Maimon to inform you of our whereabouts, but it is better that you did not have to return to Cordoba and find us gone."

"And here in Toledo?" asked Gavriel. "Are you practicing medicine again? Did the al-Jadys come with you?"

Solomon shook his head sadly. "I am now teaching medicine at the House of Science. It is part of the Academy of Toledo. But though I have found success in this city, I feel alone in my calling as never before. The al-Jadys left Cordoba also," disclosed the hakim. "They have gone to Egypt."

The news struck Gavriel a hard blow. "To Egypt? But why not here, to Toledo?"

Solomon's eyes moistened. He struggled a moment to find the right words. "The Almoravids raided our dispensary. They smashed all our medicine vials, broke our tables with axes. They forbade us to work together, to treat Muslims, Jews and Christians in the same place. Zahid wanted to get as far away from the Veiled Ones as he possibly could. He thought Egypt the likeliest place. I grieve the loss deeply."

Gavriel could not speak. It felt as if someone had yanked the lungs out of his chest.

Solomon continued, "That dispensary was my life. Its violation broke something inside of me, and I knew I could no longer live in Cordoba."

Gavriel rose and embraced his father. Then he sought a dark corner in which to lie down and weep until he sank into oblivious slumber.

The following morning a messenger arrived, summoning Solomon to the archbishop's residence. "His Excellency has a visitor," the man explained, "who has taken ill."

Solomon gathered up his things and prepared to depart.

"I'll come with you," said Gavriel.

"As you like."

The messenger had brought a horse, which Solomon rode as Gavriel walked alongside. The boy glanced up at his father. There was so much he longed to say, but how to begin? The hakim stared straight ahead, lost in his own thoughts.

The sick man lay on a gilded bed, surrounded by attendants. Hundreds of candles lit the room, for this late autumn day was gloomy. The patient smiled with relief as the Jews approached him. He was fine-boned, with a hint of silver in his hair and a vigor un-expected in someone who had taken to his sickbed.

"Thank God you're here," he said. "This boil on my hip pains me so!"

Gavriel stopped short. The voice was familiar. He had seen this man! It was the abbot from the public well in Charnay, whose entourage Garin, Bernard and Robert had deserted. The force of the coincidence nearly knocked Gavriel off his feet, but he steadied himself and whispered to Solomon, "May I examine the patient?"

Solomon nodded and took a step backward.

The abbot pulled away his bedclothes to reveal a festering boil. Gavriel inspected it closely, then felt the man's forehead. "He is feverish from the ill humors of the boil," he said. "Father, hand me the _bistoury_."

Solomon willingly took on the role of assistant

as Gavriel swabbed, lanced and bandaged the boil. If it bothered the hakim that the procedure took longer than normal because the boy paused often to close his eyes and breathe deeply, he said nothing. With evident approval he listened to his son call for wine and eggwhite, then watched him mix and brush it over the boil.

"Repeat this process twice during the night," he instructed the attendants. "I will come back tomorrow to have a look."

Father and son departed then. No words passed between them on the way home, but the comfortable silence confirmed that Solomon knew what Gavriel wished him to know, and was glad.

The next day they found Peter of Cluny seated before a great stone fireplace, drinking lustily from a cup of mead. He wore a gilded cross pendant and a silk robe over his bedclothes. "It's remarkable," he exclaimed, "how much better I feel. And it's a good thing, because I don't have time for infirmity! I've come to Spain on the Lord's business, and am needed back at Cluny as soon as I can possibly return." He flashed a grateful smile at his visitors. "Oh, you Jewish physicians! It's amazing what you can do. Allow me to apologize for my fellow Christians. As you well know, they've taken Jerusalem by sword and wrought havoc here, there and everywhere in between. If only I could stop them ... but they won't listen to me. I must try to bring about changes slowly, one small step at a time."

"Changes?" Solomon raised his eyebrows.

Peter got to his feet and allowed Gavriel to

inspect the boil. "Yes, changes. I stand firmly *against* these horrible Crusades! Christians seem to be caught in a state of foolhardy ignorance, but I believe that a man of faith can also be a man of intellect. And furthermore, I believe that the grace of Christ reaches out even to such as Jews and Muslims, if they will but receive it! After all you are, as the Mohammedans so eloquently say, People of the Book."

"Thank you just the same," said Solomon politely, "but we Jews intend to remain Jews."

Peter sighed, "Ah, but you Jews are a stubborn people! Nevertheless, the Crusades turn me cold. I prefer to fight with the mind, not the sword." He gave Solomon an inspired look. "Your people are known for scholarship. Perhaps you can help me."

"And how might I do that?"

Gavriel finished examining the boil and helped the abbot back into his seat. The man raised eager hands, explaining, "I want to know the mind of the infidel – to understand his religion so that I, and those who would follow me, can *persuade* him over to Christ rather than cut him down in violence."

Father and son glanced at one another over the abbot's head.

"I've come to Spain to hire Arabic speakers. I want them to help translate the Koran into Latin. Then I will be able to read the blasted book and gain some kind of understanding of what it is those Mohammedans believe! Are you acquainted with any educated men who might need a job?"

Solomon winked at Gavriel. "It just so happens I have a brother who finds himself in great financial need at the moment. He is educated, and fluent not only in Arabic but in many other languages."

Peter's face lit up. "And is he available?"

"Absolutely," said Gavriel. "He's ... shall we say, taking a ... *rest* from his usual vocation just now."

The abbot settled back into his chair and resumed drinking his mead. "Fine, fine! Bring him to me and I'll have a talk with him. I'm prepared to pay him for his efforts. He can stay right here in Toledo of course, but tell him he will have to work with Christians."

Gavriel bit his lip to stifle a laugh. "Oh, my uncle is well used to Christians. In fact, he spent a good portion of the summer in their company."

"Excellent. I will build a team of the finest translators imaginable! Oh, and I want to purchase an astrolabe while I'm here. Do you know where I might find one? I want the very best money can buy."

Gavriel gave the abbot an apologetic smile. "I'm sorry, Your Grace, but I don't think we can help you with that."

ॐ॰ ॐ॰ ॐ॰

The two physicians declined the offer of horses and walked home instead, wrapped in thick cloaks against the wind. They stopped on the crest of a hill and gazed down at the deep gorge cutting a path around Toledo. "I suppose," said Solomon, "that in time, we will come to feel at home in this strange city." He led Gavriel past the Academy, and showed him the synagogue in which the Zafrani family now worshipped. When they reached home, he disappeared for a few minutes and returned with something bundled in a linen sack. He handed it to Gavriel.

"Nizar intended to give you this in parting," he said. "But as you will remember, he was prevented from doing so."

Gavriel recalled only too clearly Nizar's shout, al-Jady pulling him backward, the brutish Almoravid soldier on horseback. He opened the sack and found an exquisitely carved teakwood box with sturdy lock and key. A design of birds and flowers graced the lid, inlaid with silver and ivory.

"Nizar said it was to hold all the money you made from trading. But I think perhaps, it might hold your most precious medicines instead. Every hakim should have such a box."

Gavriel felt strangely shy as he lifted his eyes to his father's face. "You never gave up on me."

"Does the Almighty give up on the Jewish people?" Solomon replied. "Surely he expects a father to do no less for his only son. But I admit, your uncle has made this job much easier for me. Reuven has been far from silent about the danger and hardship you faced in the Rhinelands. He's told me more than once how you met it all with courage and resolve. Gavriel, you have earned a father's pride. And now the struggles you have overcome will only serve to make you a more skilled and determined physician. The privilege will be mine to serve beside you."

Gavriel opened the box and breathed deeply of the rich wood scent. He closed it again and ran a reverent hand over the lid's contours. How he wished Nizar could see him now! He knew the Arab youth would rejoice with him in this moment of victory. Blessed be the jeweled astrolabe, wherever it was! Its loss had brought immeasurable gain.

THE END

GLOSSARY OF TERMS

abbot	a man who is the head of a monastery
al-Andalus	ARABIC – the part of Spain ruled by Muslims
Allah	ARABIC – God
al-Maghrib	modern day Morocco, Tunisia and Algeria
Almohads	strongly fundamentalist Berber Muslims, who emphasized the "Oneness" of Allah
Almoravids	fundamentalist Berber Muslims
amber	a pale yellow, brownish or reddish fossil resin used to make jewelry or other ornamentation
astrolabe	an astronomical instrument used for measuring the altitude of sun and stars
Berber	a North African tribe
bishop	one who oversees all the churches of a certain district

burnoose	a hooded cloak worn by Arabs and Berbers
bistoury	a long, narrow surgical knife
caliph	a muslim ruler
camphor	a medicine obtained from the camphor tree, used to soothe irritated or infected skin
Crusades	a series of wars in the 11th, 12th and 13th centuries in which European Christians fought for control of the Holy Lands
cupping glass	a heated glass used to draw blood to the skin's surface through suction
denier	a French silver coin
dhimmi	Arabic name for non-Muslims who are "people of the book" (Jews and Christians)
dhow	ARABIC – traditional Arab sailing vessel
dirham	silver coin used in al-Andalus
ell	a measure of length equalling 45 inches
emir	A muslim ruler claiming descent from the prophet Mohammed
esparto	a type of grass native to southern Europe and North Africa
galley	an ancient, Mediterranean seagoing vessel propelled by oars

gangrene	death of soft tissue due to obstructed circulation
hazzan	A Jewish singer who leads prayer in the synagogue
hemp	a tall, coarse plant, the fibers of which are used for making rope
jute	a strong, coarse fiber used to make sacks
khamisa	ARABIC – a long-sleeved, loose shirt
kosher	fit or allowed to be eaten or used according to Jewish dietary laws
Levant	the countries bordering on the eastern Mediterranean Sea from Turkey to Egypt
maristan	a public hospital, usually attached to a mosque
matzoh	a brittle, flat piece of unleavened bread
mercenary	a professional soldier who fights merely for money or other reward
mitzvah	HEBREW – any good or praiseworthy deed
Mozarab	Arabic-speaking Christians in Spain
mullah	a Muslim religious leader
nagid	leader of a Sephardic Jewish community
pilah	a dish in which grain (rice or wheat) is browned in oil then cooked in broth

Sefarad	the Hebrew name for Spain
sephardic jew	a Jew from Spain or Portugal
shalom	a Hebrew greeting or farewell, meaning "peace"
Shema Yisrael	HEBREW – "Hear, oh Israel", the first two words of the central declaration of Jewish faith in one God, recited both morning and night (The complete Shema includes Deuteronomy 6:4-9, 11:13-21 and Numbers 14:37-41)
Silk Road	an ancient trade route between China and the Mediterranean Sea, extending 4,000 miles
shohet	HEBREW – a kosher butcher
Talmud	the collection of Jewish law and tradition produced in ancient Babylonia
Templar	a military order founded by crusaders around A.D. 1118
tonsure	the part of a monk's head left bare by shaving the hair
Torah	the first five books of the Bible

Jennifer Johnson Garrity

...grew up in Portland, Oregon but has lived in Europe for about twenty years. She currently resides in southern Germany with her husband and two of her three children. Jennifer is also the author of *The Bushwhacker* (Peachtree Pub. Ltd. 1999), *Et Sted i Hjertet* (Danish - Hovedland, 2003), *Calendar Quest* (BrimWood Press, 2006) and *Family Tree* (BrimWood Press, 2006).

Lee Fitzgerrell Smith, B.A., M.F.A.

...has designed giftware, created stationery collections, artistic signage, and painted murals for homes and businesses, along with illustrating a television commercial. Her artwork has appeared in books, magazines, and corporate publications. One of her favorite things to do, however, is illustrate books and add creative images to exciting words.

Kelsey Garrity

...grew up in Belgium and Germany, and is currently studying art in Savannah, Georgia. She has also illustrated *Calendar Quest* (BrimWood Press, 2006) and *Color the Western World* (BrimWood Press, 2006).